Richard Owain Roberts wa   and
now lives in Cardiff, Wales   at
the University of Manche   reative
Writing MA programme at LJMU. His fiction and non-fiction
has appeared in a variety of places in print, online, and radio.
This is his debut short-story collection.

Follow Richard on Twitter @RichOwainRobs

www.richardowainroberts.com

All The Places We Lived

All The Places We Lived

Stories by
Richard Owain Roberts

Parthian, Cardigan SA43 1ED
www.parthianbooks.com
First published in 2015
© Richard Owain Roberts 2015
ISBN 978-1-910409-65-7
Editor: Susie Wild
Cover design by Katherine Hardy (http://kardy.org)
Typeset by Elaine Sharples
Printed and bound by Gomer Press
Published with the financial support of the Welsh Books Council
British Library Cataloguing in Publication Data
A cataloguing record for this book is available from the British Library.

For Amy

All The Places We Lived

DISNEYLAND

Happy New Year, Robert. We are very grateful for your hard work over the course of the last year, this effort did not go unnoticed. We feel this great relationship can go on from strength to strength. We have carefully selected seven hundred tasks for you to complete over the course of this year and are sure they will be completed to the best possible standard, setting a fantastic precedent for the rest of the year! Yours faithfully.

Robert closes his laptop and looks at his iPhone. The clock reads 4.30 a.m. Robert thinks,

This is fantastic news.

Robert walks into the bedroom. His wife, Eva, is asleep. Eva is snoring. Eva quit her job as a social worker six months ago and in the last six months has,

a new tattoo (pizza slice outline)

a new tattoo (cat on a bicycle)

read Richard Yates (the novel)
read Richard Yates (the writer)

improved her core strength via the pull-up bar (monkeying technique) improved her core strength via the pull-up bar (windscreen wiper technique).

Eva deleted her Facebook two months ago and told Robert that every day is the best possible excuse to feel good about living. Robert looks at Eva and puts his hands on his head. Robert closes his eyes for a moment and forgets that he is standing up; his legs buckle a little before his regains his balance and opens his eyes. It is dark outside, and windy. The windows rattle a little. Robert thinks,

This sound is okay, I should record this sound.

Robert picks up his iPhone and stretches his arm out towards the window, recording. Robert leaves the bedroom and walks downstairs and into the kitchen. Robert and Eva live in west Wales. The house they live in was described by the estate agent as needing 'complete modernisation throughout'. When they looked round the house for the first time, Eva said that all of her dreams were coming true in realtime. The estate agent asked Eva what she meant by the term realtime, Eva looked at the estate agent and said, Will they accept the asking price?

Robert and Eva moved into the house with their cat, Arnold, and a bullmastiff puppy called Moses. The animals have contrasting personalities but get along nicely. Robert told Eva that he finds most people's personalities leave him numb. Eva told Robert that she finds most people's personalities leave her disappointed. Eva sometimes talks about how she perceives herself to be an unpopular person. Robert tells Eva: it's you that doesn't like them.

They paid four hundred thousand pounds for the house and this meant they had eight hundred pounds left over to complete renovation work. The house is made up of,

a hallway which leads off to,

a large living room that has an open fireplace at either end
a small snug
a large, square kitchen that has original floor tiling dating back to the late nineteenth century

The staircase is old and creaks, it leads up towards,

a large bedroom
a large bedroom
a small bedroom
a bathroom
a small bedroom.

All of Robert and Eva's furniture and possessions from their old house fit inside the large living room. On their first day in the new house, Robert and Eva ate a packet of plain wholemeal wraps at 8 p.m. Eva said, This is the first time in a new place that we haven't ordered Domino's on the first night.

Robert said, Domino's hell lifestyle.

Robert sits down at the kitchen table and runs both his hands up and down the tabletop. The table was a gift from his mother, it cost five hundred pounds at auction. The table is old and beautiful and won't ever break. Robert eats two Weetabix with soya milk from a chipped brown tapas bowl. It is very quiet in the kitchen. Moses is asleep. Robert's iPhone vibrates.

Dear Robert, please can you confirm receipt of our last email to you, dated January fourth, 4 a.m. This is so we know you understand the forthcoming schedule of tasks. Yours faithfully.

Robert puts the iPhone down and runs both hands up and down the tabletop. Robert is unable to lift his hands. He needs to lift his hands from the tabletop to be able to stand up. Standing up is an essential first step towards returning to the small bedroom. Once in the small bedroom, Robert will be able to contact his employer to confirm that he is making a start on his task. The first task of the year. January the fourth, 4.30 a.m.

Eva walks into the small bedroom and says, What are you doing?

Robert turns and looks at Eva, she is wearing grey tracksuit bottoms. Robert says, I'm editing footage and then putting it back together again. Sometimes the footage has to be at a slower speed, or sometimes it has to be looped, or sometimes it has to be in negative. I'm not sure if this is what editing is, I think it's what they want.

Eva stretches her arms above her head and clasps her hands together momentarily. Eva says, How long have you been up?

Robert says, Three hours.

Eva walks towards Robert and kisses him on his forehead. Robert rests his head on Eva's shoulder. Eva picks up a T-shirt from the floor and puts it on. The T-shirt has N. W. A. written on the front in large black lettering. Eva says, If Eazy-E was still alive it would be a good reality show for him to live in west Wales, maybe something to do with canoes or abseiling. No?

Robert nods his head and presses cmd+v on the keyboard. He presses cmd+v four times in succession which makes four, three second, identical clips. Robert presses cmd+o and selects to slow the first clip down by ten percent. Robert presses cmd+o and selects to slow the second clip down by twenty percent. Robert presses cmd+o and selects to slow the third clip down by sixty percent. Robert looks at the screen and shuts his eyes.

Eva puts her hands on Robert's shoulder and squeezes a blackhead.

* * *

June the fifteenth, Robert and Eva look at Facebook.

Imagine being with someone who thought it was appropriate to put photos of food on here. Am I a bad person?

No. Is food worse than rhetorical question statuses?

Yes. No. What will you write if I die?

I'll write. I don't know, um... maybe I'll update your profile picture with a Cambodian skull.

5

But what will you write? This really needs to be agreed upon.

Okay, um… Eternal sleep, with no conscious thought, my body burnt and scattered in a humanist ceremony? Don't mind if I do!

Lol.

If anyone writes anything underneath, I'll write, um… who are you, you're next, or, um… it can death.

Lol. It can death.

Oh. Someone from my PGCE deleted me.

Lol, cold.

She had Asperger's, or she said she had Asperger's.

Message her and ask why.

Okay.

* * *

Moses is now nine months old, it is August the nineteenth. Most mornings Moses and Robert walk and run together through the woods beyond the bottom of the back garden. To get there they walk through two fields, a small unkempt apple orchard, and another field.

6

Robert stops walking and breaks a dead branch from a tree and holds it in front of his face like a sword. Moses circles Robert and jumps up and down, barking. Your bark sounds funny when you jump, Moses, Robert says. Robert looks beyond the branch and sees a man looking back at him. The man, a farmer maybe, has a gun resting on his shoulder.

Hello.

You can't be here, this is private land.

I didn't realise, sorry. Is it your land?

No, I look after it. You can't be here, it's privately owned.

Okay. I don't know, it just doesn't seem like it's a problem me being here.

The man takes his gun and points it towards Moses and says, That dog.

Robert sighs. He is wearing a grey T-shirt and yellow shorts. He can feel sweat running down his back, his heart is beating very quickly. Moses, Moses, Moses, Robert says. He puts the dog on his lead and they turn and walk.

They move quickly through the field and once they reach the orchard Robert stops and lets Moses off his lead. Robert picks a rotting apple and shouts, Fucker. He throws the apple in the direction of the woods. Robert says, Moses Moses Moses. Robert and Moses run without pause until they arrive at the gate at the bottom of the garden.

Eva is in the garden with Arnold and Moses. Arnold is lying on a piece of rotting wood and Moses is rolling in a puddle. Eva says, You guys, what are you doing? Eva looks at the outbuilding and shouts, We should turn this into a space for guests, we should turn this into a space for guests.

Where?

The outbuilding.

Okay.

Eva picks up a tennis ball and throws it up in the air. She looks up and loses sight of the ball in the sun. She thinks:

I don't know.

Eva walks over to the pond to look at tadpoles. Eva looks at her reflection in the water and shouts, Am I still a babe, am I still a babe, am I still a babe?

Yes, more so, more so, Robert shouts, his voice breaking, upbeat and emotional.

* * *

The house being exposed to the elements means there is constant upkeep required to ensure comfortable and tidy living. It is November.

Robert and Eva climb a ladder and sit on the roof so they can replace broken and damaged slate. Eva looks at her hands and smiles. Your eyes look more Asian than usual, Robert says.

Eva points towards the clouds and the sun and then towards a bird, a heron. Heron, Eva says.

Robert puts his hands on the collar of his T-shirt and pulls down. Heron, Robert says, Heron flow from the eighties. Heron and heron. That's a homophone.

Robert stops pulling and lets his hands hang from the collar. He looks at the heron, When I was eight I went to Disneyland, Florida. Sam and I were waiting to get served food at one of the stalls, donuts or something. Sam started talking to the man in front of us in the queue. Eazy-E. The man was Eric Wright. Eric Wright. Eazy-E from N. W. A.! They talked and then Eric Wright said, What up nigga, want a photo. Sam said, Thank you, I'm a fan. Oh, This is my little brother, Robert. Eazy-E said, Young buck, nice to meet you. I wrapped my arms around Sam's leg and pressed my face into his thigh. Sam and Eric Wright, Eazy-E, laughed. I opened my eyes and smiled a little. I remember feeling the urge to start dancing, I don't know if that's a real memory or not. It doesn't matter. Eric Wright, Eric Wright's girlfriend, Sam and I stood and smiled and we had our picture taken. Eric Wright and Eric Wright's girlfriend took their food order and left. Sam looked at me and asked me if I knew who Eric Wright was, who Eazy-E was. I started crying because I recognised him but didn't know his name. I felt humiliated, but Sam said it was okay. Sam said, They took the photo on their camera, that's funny, that's a really funny thing to happen.

Summer Trip (Annual) (Commemorative)

Steven Gravelle, David Gravelle and Trystan Gravelle go camping for one week every summer, the end of July until the first of August, to commemorate the death of their grandfather. Their grandfather did nothing special, he wasn't an individual of any particular renown but he wasn't a bad person either. He made an effort and never gave up in situations where many people may have done. That is the popular opinion. He died of cancer, a slow and complex death. It doesn't matter. Steven Gravelle, David Gravelle and Trystan Gravelle will all also die eventually. Maybe one of them will die of cancer too. It doesn't matter.

Fuck it, Trystan picked up his tent pole and threw it into the next sand dune. David laughed. Steven laughed.

Was that worth it? Steven said. Steven is older than Trystan. Steven is also older than David. Steven is married with three kids and feels okay most of the time. Steven does not consider himself to have ever been indulged. He has had to work hard to make money, and now feels financially comfortable. Amongst other recent purchases, Steven has come into possession of an antique motorcycle. The motorcycle is not really an antique in the true sense of the word. It is an old motorcycle. Old and antique are not the same thing. The previous owner decorated it with sprayed-on stencils of a

Native American dream catcher and an Apache chief in profile. Steven is popular in his neighbourhood, people view him as funny and kind-hearted and no one says anything derogatory about his motorcycle. When his mother died, Steven lived with his grandfather for several years that would be best summarised as 'chaotic.'

Trystan kicked into the edge of the dune and let out a cry. He is younger than Steven and younger than David. He is thirty and married to Lleucu, twenty-four, an Attachment Parenting practitioner and Psychology PhD student. Trystan was sacked from his last office job for using company time to write a seven thousand word essay, published via Google Docs, on Coronation Street's Evil David Platt. When he was eight his mother was involved in a car crash that resulted in her being comatose for two and a half months. Six months later, his father was also involved in a car crash, dying instantly. On hearing the news, Trystan began screaming and throwing books at everyone in the room. His mother said:

let him

His family stood still, sad and sympathetic looks fixed on their faces, allowing the Rupert Bear annuals to hit them on their heads, midriffs, and groins.

* * *

They began drinking. Trystan unpacked thirty-six 250ml cans of Little Hobo Czech craft lager and wanted to talk about whether Steven and David had any opinion of him marrying someone significantly younger. He was keen to know their opinions, though was also aware he would almost certainly disregard anything that was not what he wanted to hear.

Steven removed his glasses and cleaned them on his shorts, I don't think it matters what I think because it wasn't a real wedding, it wasn't legally binding.

Trystan didn't look up, Do you two ever text each other? You never text me.

No, both replied, simultaneously.

David finished his can and held his hand out for another, You get married if you want, or don't, do what makes you happy, mate, he said.

Trystan gritted his teeth, I am married. It was a proper wedding. We made a commitment.

Okay, you are married. It was a real wedding, David opened his can and drank maybe a third of it. He drank another third. Gwenno and Dad were happy, I think, so I suppose it can work. He was private, so—. David picked up his can, finished it, and looked over its design (minimalist, aspirational) and laughed.

Steven finished a beer and held the can in front of his face, Stop tweeting about beer, it's fucking embarrassing. Please pass me another beer.

Trystan passed Steven another beer, I didn't know you look at my Twitter.

Trystan closed his eyes and fell asleep on the deckchair, the last word he heard was Jesus. He woke up an hour later and made crisp sandwiches for everyone.

Steven, David, and Trystan decided that the next morning they would swim in the ocean.

* * *

David woke first and made enough scrambled eggs for the three of them. He felt happiest early in the morning. He shook the eggs from the frying pan and onto each plate. David looked at the plates and used a fork to move the eggs around so that they were distributed evenly. He shouted, Eggs, and sat down on one of the chairs they left out last night. It must have rained at some point between two and six, he felt his bum getting damp. He sighed, continued eating, continued shouting, Eggs, every couple of minutes.

Trystan opened his eyes and immediately felt conscious of how dry his mouth was. He stared up at the orange ceiling of his tent and imagined that outside of the tent was a never-ending landscape, populated only by identical unoccupied orange tents, each with its own supply of Brecon Carreg, Welch's Purple Grape juice, and bags of zip-locked mixed nuts. Trystan thought again of the barren landscape and added in a tropical greenery and two large moons in the sky. He said Predators out loud and thought of Adrien Brody (the actor) and Adrien

14

Brody (the Marie Calloway short story). Trystan heard David shout, Eggs, and opened his eyes. He looked at the orange ceiling for a moment before shutting his eyes again.

* * *

Steven, David, and Trystan stood in a row, barefoot, and looked out onto the sea. It looked okay; grey and irritable, but okay. Three years ago David had a waterproof cover (not waterproof) over his broken right arm. Four years ago Trystan was only two days back from running a marathon with an ex-girlfriend. One, two, three, four, five years ago Steven did not want to swim. It was cold and drizzling.

Trystan ran his fingers through his hair and then his beard, My beard smells metallic, I think.

The drizzle was relentless. David gave the command, a ten to one countdown, and they ran into the sea; David diving first, followed by Steven, followed by Trystan.

Trystan did not enjoy diving, he had learnt the orthodox procedure for breathing underwater only six weeks ago in the swimming pool of the Grecian villa Lleucu and he had stayed in. He splashed into the sea awkwardly and despite David and Steven already swimming ahead, he grimaced and he felt his face flush red with embarrassment.

David, well ahead of Steven, who had now been overtaken by Trystan, shouted, The race is to the buoy and back.

The buoy was barely visible in the rain. The buoy was fighting to survive. The buoy would be fine. The race was to the buoy and back.

The rain was heavy, cold, and painful. From the shore it would have been difficult to see anything other than the outline of their arms pushing past their ears and down onto the water.

David reached the buoy first and slapped both hands down on it. Breathing hard, he turned and strained his eyes to make out Trystan and Steven and then shouted, To the buoy and back, before beginning the return leg.

Having raced Lleucu every morning of their holiday (swam seven, lost four, won three – the last three), Trystan found his strength in the water much improved from previous years. Gradually, certainly, he was catching up with David. As they approached the shore he considered some kind of last minute psychological gamesmanship. He opened his mouth to shout abuse but swallowed a large amount of seawater, instantly killing all momentum.

David stood up in the water and ran to the pile of towels, T-shirts and sweaters.

Trystan stood up in the water and ran to the pile of towels, T-shirts and sweaters.

David turned back towards the sea and strained his eyes.

They walked towards the sea.

They kept walking, the water up to tops of their calves.

It's to the buoy and back, the buoy and back, Trystan shouted. What's he doing? I don't know what he's doing—

David looked on for a moment and then turned around and returned to the shore. The rain, on the beach at least, had returned to a faint drizzle, the kind that is barely perceptible, albeit soaks you nonetheless. Trystan stared as Steven continued to swim, now well beyond the buoy. Instinctively he moved his hand to his side, to locate his iPhone, to call Lleucu.

* * *

They sat on a large tree trunk surrounded by used foil barbecue trays and watched as Steven's semi-distant figure appeared to turn around. It was unclear whether this was his intention or something insisted upon by the sea. Gradually, and with sluggish consistency, he appeared closer and closer until it became evident that his appendages were no longer propellants, his head bobbing up and down, his colourful arms like forty-year-old sticks of Blackpool rock.

David stood up and walked, then ran towards, into, the sea. He lifted Steven up and dragged him to the shore before placing him in the recovery position. David watched as Steven stirred momentarily before throwing up, repeatedly.

Trystan put his hands down to his sides. Trystan lifted his hands over his head. Trystan retched, threw up into his hands, and then onto the beach.

* * *

Pulling a four pack of Tyskie beer from the coolbox and passing one to Steven and throwing the other to David, Trystan opened his bottle and drank maybe half, They're small bottles. Small bottles, but I like them. Did you turn around, did you choose to turn around? Basically, that's what I want to know: did you choose to turn around or were you turned around?

Steven smiled and said, What difference does it make? I'm here now.

Trystan felt his bottom lip trembling and he dug the nail of his index finger into his thumb, Dramatic wanker—

Steven was laughing, but only a little. He stopped laughing, Fuck off you little prince. He ran his hands through his hair, pushing it back, exposing his forehead, his receding hairline, small scars from his youth. Dramatic? That's very funny, that's very funny. I'm assuming you're being serious, that you're earnestly angry at me when you say that.

Trystan looked into the fire, Don't abuse me.

Steven leaned forward in his chair. He ran his hands through his hair again. He leaned back in his chair, What could I possibly say now that isn't going to result in hours and hours of you moaning like a dickless six-year-old? I chose to turn around. I wasn't trying to kill myself, obviously that's not what I was doing... and, for reference, you never need to email me about this incident, or anything you think might have led to this incident. Stop sending me that kind of email. Stop emailing me at all, actually. 'Summer Trip' brackets 'Annual' brackets 'Commemorative', what kind of, what, what planet are you from? Don't talk to me about your problems, it's boring.

Trystan sat up in his chair and looked at David and then looked at Steven. Fuck you, abuser, he said, struggling to retain any kind of composure.

Steven adjusted his glasses, focused, then threw his can at Trystan's head. The can struck just above his left eyebrow and split the skin on impact. Blood began to trickle down Trystan's face. He put his hand to the cut, dabbed it, then rose up and lunged wildly towards Steven, who became unbalanced in his chair and fell backwards, kicking his legs out and catching Trystan in the mouth. Trystan grabbed Steven's right foot and bit his big toe—

* * *

David was the first to wake. David was always the first to wake. He took his tent down and packed it up quietly and efficiently before making a start on the scrambled eggs. David was too young to remember living with his grandfather in the years following his and Steven's mother's death, and by the time their father died he had experienced enough in his life to see death as something that merely happens and doesn't involve, in practical terms, as much trauma as it is traditionally afforded:

for example, a shitty relationship is more traumatic than dying (you or someone you know).

David recalled an email Trystan sent him:

Hi. I didn't meet granddad (you already know this) so I feel like I'm less related to him than other people who knew him (you, for example). Can you tell me some things about him. I don't think he'd like me, I can't imagine what we'd talk about. Does that matter? I still think these trips are a good idea. Steven never replies to my emails. Bye.

David tried to remember his response:

I don't think it matters. Try and relax, something something something something—

David couldn't remember the response.

David looked at the eggs, they were cooking perfectly. He turned them over in the pan, said, Eggs, and walked into the woods to collect firewood to take home with him.

Marmaris, Turkey

Jaimie's skin is darker than normal. My skin is darker than normal. Our skins are darker than normal. Our skins are darker than normal due to the hot climate and because we have been lying underneath the sun for six hours every day for the last two weeks. We have been applying sun cream at regular intervals but we cannot stop the sun from changing how we look. Jaimie states that being in the sun makes her feel happier than normal:

I feel happier than normal because of the sun.

The hotel has a jetty that stretches out over the sea. We jump off the jetty steps four times a day and swim for twenty minutes each time. There is a red and green buoy about one hundred meters from the jetty and we race to it. Jaimie has won most of the races because her technique is cleaner and because I tend to give up and start laughing at around the halfway point.

I tell Jaimie that it is time to race:

It is time to race. I expect a keenly fought contest. Don't fuck with me.

Jaimie tells me that she is ready to race and beat her personal best:

I am ready to race. I am ready to beat my PB into the fuckin' ground.

I tell Jaimie, Go!, and start swimming. I look at the buoy and think:

Concentrate on your goal and not on Jaimie.

Approaching fifty metres we are equal, but I feel strong and confident. After seventy-five metres I am focusing only on touching the buoy. I think:

I am determined.

I touch the buoy and turn around.

Jaimie is five metres behind me and keeps swimming until she touches the buoy. She slaps her hand down on it and laughs.

Jaimie smiles and kisses me on the lips. Jaimie complements me on my victory in between completing forward roles. We play a game where we try to balance on the rope that runs from the buoy back to the jetty. We tread water and talk about the other people on the jetty, the hotel staff, and about the possibility of hiring segways.

We swim back to the jetty.

* * *

It is cocktail hour in the hotel. I ask the barman for two cocktails and whilst he is making them he tells me that he doesn't like the music they play in the bar. His name is Georghe. Georghe tells me that his passion is rap music and he is going to put on some Turkish hip hop the first chance he gets. He asks me what I would be doing if I wasn't on holiday.

I don't know what to say.

Georghe says, Come on, man. Come on, come on, come on!

I tell him that I would be drinking tap water and thinking about times when I didn't say what I wanted to say to people and ended up regretting it.

The barman smiles and tells me that I should blackmail a rich person and when I have enough money, kill the rich person. Georghe says, Gotta make that cash money. I don't know what is going on with Georghe, and why he is doing an American accent. I want to ask him about his personal life, but he starts talking about blackmail and murder again.

I ask Georghe if I have to kill the rich person. He says that it is up to me but, personally, he would kill the rich person. I ask Georghe if he is talking from personal experience.

Georghe, the barman, the hip hop fan, the murderer, hands me two cocktails.

* * *

We are walking along the boulevard in Marmaris, Turkey. Jaimie is looking at the boats and points at one that is for sale for nine hundred thousand euros. There are people up on the deck of the nine hundred thousand euro boat and they are all smiling and laughing intermittently. It is our last night here and we do not have enough money left over to buy two beers.

A waiter steps out from a restaurant and tells us that his is the best restaurant in Marmaris. The waiter is tall and has straight, white teeth. The waiter tells me that I am a very handsome man and I will enjoy his restaurant.

I tell the waiter that I have no money and I have already eaten tonight.

The waiter tells Jaimie that her husband is a very handsome man and would enjoy his restaurant. He is saying, Why not, over and over.

Jaimie tells the waiter that we have no money and have already eaten tonight.

The waiter believes this and tells us that we are a very good-looking couple and we can come in for one round of drinks.

I tell the waiter that we do not have enough money for one round of drinks but if we did, we would come in for one round of drinks.

The waiter believes me and tells us that he would love to see us both at his restaurant tomorrow evening for a meal and some drinks.

I tell the waiter that tonight is our last night here.

The waiter's teeth are straight, and white. The waiter's teeth disappear. The waiter puts his hand up a waves goodbye and tells us that one day, if we come back to Marmaris, he would like us to come to his restaurant for a meal and some drinks. The waiter is tall and has straight white teeth. His teeth have returned and this is comforting, somehow.

Jaimie puts her hand around my waist, Why didn't you just say we'd come back tomorrow? He seemed upset.

He was upset, he didn't believe me. Then he believed me. Then he felt better. That's how you succeed in living an extreme honesty lifestyle, I say.

Extreme honesty lifestyle holiday.

Nine hundred thousand euro boat extreme purchase-culture holiday.

There's a cruise ship that is also an apartment block where prices range from three million dollars to forty million dollars.

Just get me a forty million dollar cruise ship apartment you lazy bum.

Extreme cruise ship purchase decision. Maybe we could live on a houseboat?

No. I only ever want to live on land.

Jaimie rolls her eyes for affect, Landlubber lifestyle.

Landlubber lifestyle, I say, feeling calm and tanned.

* * *

Two ginger cats are lying next to each other on the ramp leading up to a small fishing boat.

Boat-cat lifestyle.

Boat-cat holiday lifestyle.

A medium-sized tabby cat is lying, eyes closed, by the side of a large potted plant. Jaimie and I look at each other.

Chillbomber cat.

Snoozebomber cat.

A large tabby cat is walking very slowly towards some bushes. It has a suspicious facial expression. Jaimie and I look at each other and narrow our eyes.

Stealth cat.

Police state cat.

A ginger and white cat is sitting next to a table of four people. The people are dropping pieces of food for the cat. The cat looks at the food then walks away, laughing. Jaimie and I look at each other and high five without touching.

Prank cat.

Original Bart Simpson Attitude cat.

* * *

Jaimie stops walking and looks at me, When I was six we went to Santorini, Greece and I saw a waiter throwing a cat off the edge of a cliff. They were throwing cats into the sea because the cats were bothering them. I was sad for the cats and I was scared because I thought they might pick me up and throw me with them. I wizzed myself. I didn't even try to stop it happening, we had to leave the restaurant. My parents were very nice about it, they didn't mention the wizzing. We went for an ice cream on the boulevard. Next year we went to Jamaica, and they bought me Whiskas from the supermarket and let me feed the stray cats every day. I don't know, that's just something that happened. Jaimie stops talking and stares at an empty tour boat.

I don't know which part of the story to react to. Jaimie is saner now compared to when we first met. I am saner now compared to when we first met. It really doesn't matter which part of the story I react to.

I look down at the floor, I won't let anyone throw you off a cliff.

Jaimie holds my hand, I won't let anyone throw you off a cliff.

Barcelona, Catalunya

A Japanese man is washing a large red tomato in the bathroom of an unfinished Gaudi cathedral. He is determined to do well in this task. Completing tasks is his primary form of expression and it makes him happy. He looks like he means business and has my best wishes.

The cathedral has a quiet area that leads to a silent area. This is where people go to transmit their hopes and opinions to God. People are smiling, there is an unequivocal belief that God is here and, furthermore, is pleased to see everyone.

The queue for the gift shop is twenty to thirty people long. I queue for forty minutes and buy one Gaudi pencil and one Gaudi eraser. Other people buy similar products:

Gaudi pencil case—

Gaudi photo frame—

Gaudi marbles—

Everyone is speaking in different languages:

German, Italian, English, Japanese, maybe Dutch.

Most people are here in pairs, they are travelling together, existing in each other's space:

happily, gladly.

Someone, a boy in his late teens, passes me a large and expensive-looking camera and asks if I can take a photo of him and his friend. I try to explain that I don't think photography is permitted, but the teenage boy looks confused so I take the photograph anyway. He says, Merci. I say, Merci.

The people in the silent area are still transmitting their feelings. How long it takes may depend on what an individual requires, and how urgently. This is very serious, anything could happen. Anything could happen at any minute in this extreme cathedral environment. If God decides that we are fucked, destined to die here and now, then that's it: it's happening. It's happening and we need to accept it.

* * *

I wait in line for access to a balcony. I stop waiting after one hour. I could have taken a photo or a short video up on the balcony; I could have captured something, recorded exactly what was going on in the unfinished Gaudi cathedral at this precise moment in time. I struggle to remember things unless I take a photo or make a short video recording. I only enjoy accessing memories in the post-edit stage and this is easier to do through the use of technology than it is through the mind.

* * *

I feel warm and look at my iPhone to check the temperature. I eat a small handful of pumpkin seeds. I stare at the most recently added parts of the outer structure of the cathedral and think:

Feels incoherent.

* * *

We lived in Berlin. We were together for five or six years, four of those married. Berlin was okay, our relationship was okay. On the day the divorce papers came through, I commented that:

You are entirely to blame for this, no, I don't mean that, but I'd say sixty:forty, sixty five:thirty five.

We left all of our stuff in the apartment and were charged three and a half thousand euros to have it removed. I emailed the agent and asked if the furniture and clothes could be donated to charity. I copied Orla into the email and she replied:

Agree with this sentiment.

* * *

I walk down a side street and into Bar Pastís. My Catalan is much better than it was, I feel like I notice an improvement once every three months. The barman, Gerard, says that I look nervous today. He says this in Catalan and then in English, but the two versions don't seem to match exactly and I'm not certain I know what he means. I ask him for an Estrella and offer him one. I sit at the bar and we drink and talk about the best registas that have existed post nineteen ninety-five.

Gerard's shift finishes and instead of sitting with me he says he has to meet his friend to arrange the purchase of a new bicycle. He puts his hand on my shoulder and mumbles something about fixed gears, before leaving. I get up from the bar and sit on a stool by the window at the front of the bar. I drink half of my Estrella and look at the Estrella next to it, full.

* * *

I blocked Orla on Facebook when we divorced. She emailed me and said this was a good idea, that she approved of my actions, that she had considered doing the same thing but didn't want to come across as aggressive. She asked me:

Are you happy? Feel like the reason it didn't work was because, like, you didn't ever switch off maybe. Are you still like that? Did me not being in your life change that, was it my fault, was I provoking that aspect of your personality? It doesn't matter now, whatever. What do you do every day when you wake up? How do you fill your time? Do you still obsess over sports? We used to watch trailers on IMDB, do you remember that? That was a thing we did on Saturday mornings. Do you do that still? Where do you live? Are you happy? I want you to be happy.

I didn't reply to the email. I filed the it under 'Orla', itself a subfile of 'Other.' Other Orla. Oral Other. There was no broadband where I was living and I only used the internet for maybe half an hour each day at Starbucks. I tried to Google Orla once but nothing came up and it seemed astonishing to me that she had absolutely no internet presence. I set up a fake Facebook and tried to search for her but found nothing. I thought maybe she was dead, then I laughed—

* * *

I look at my watch and it's 11.30 p.m. A friend I know from my apartment building is sitting across from me. We're still drinking Estrella but he's brought over two absinthe with him.

I say Jesus in Welsh, Catalan, and English.

Artur laughs and says Jesus in Catalan, Welsh and English.

Artur brings over two more absinthe. He tells me about how after school he used to cruise the neighbourhood with friends on the look out for Spanish flags and when they found one they would take it down and smear it in dog shit. I tell him I approve and we laugh, high five, and then hug. I'm crying a little. We drink the absinthe.

I lose consciousness.

* * *

I wake and throw up over the side of my mattress.

I lose consciousness. In my dream I imagine that I'm inside the internet. Being inside of the internet is okay. It is perhaps not as aesthetically appealing as Tron, but it's fine. A large fox runs past me and I jump towards him, trying to grab a hold of his tail. I miss, and fall down a hole. It's fine, I'm not hurt. Laughing hysterically as I do, I start shouting:

I want my minority report.

An infinite number of tabs open up in front of my eyes and they slowly close in on me, creeping, but with unabashed determination of purpose. I close my eyes and wait—

* * *

Orla was always trying to appease everyone in her life. People would comment about her generosity of spirit, her kindness. Her father punched her in the stomach once, twisted her arm possibly two or three times, other stuff maybe, but she forgave him and cooked his breakfast on Sundays. He was a piece of shit. Orla understood this, instinctively she got it. She felt if she could make him a little happier, he might be happy on his own one day.

We would argue sometimes about how I thought Orla needed to call people out on their bullshit more often. Including her father. Including me:

If you don't understand by this point when, how, I need your

33

help... just, please stop being so fucking indecisive and take control of yourself—

* * *

I walk back to Bar Pastís. It's four in the afternoon, maybe twenty-six or twenty-seven degrees. I take a seat at the bar and Gerard pours me an Estrella. We talk about prison escape movies and beard oil. I ask Gerard if he likes the Old Faithful sample I gave him. Gerard smiles, nods, and pours me another Estrella. I take it and sit on the stool by the front window. I think about:

How I always confuse the word mirror with the word window.

My first instinct is always to process them as being different words for the same thing.

I ask Gerard for another Estrella.

* * *

The MNAC is my favourite place in the city. I get off the bus and walk up the path, past the main entrance and stand in front of the snack bar. I order a pancake. I order a mojito. It's busy today, there aren't many spaces to sit, but I find one next to some Japanese students. The students appear tired, maybe they're jaded and bored in this alien environment, I don't know. I look across to them and say:

私たちはここになりまし底から開始

My Japanese is poor. I couldn't hold a conversation, but I have an understanding of the most basic of basics. The students seems impressed, but I don't catch what they say back to me. I finish eating the pancake and get up to go inside.

I am inside for three hours. I look at:

Mattisse
Pere Serra
Jaume Huguet
Bernat Martorell
Francisco de Zurbarán

I stop and look at the Picassos. I find my favourite:

a portrait of Dora Maar.

This used to be the background on my MacBook. Orla didn't like it, she used to say:

Picasso. More like Picrappo.

I'm conscious of how hard I'm staring. I want to keep on staring. I want to stare harder. I want to start head-butting Dora Maar, keeping my eyes open the whole time. Dora Maar is ambivalent, jolly even. Picrappo. I start laughing. I think I'm laughing. I definitely am laughing.

Someone is standing behind me.

Picrappo—

Someone is putting their hand on my shoulder.

Picrappo—

Picrappo—

Someone is saying hello. Someone is saying hello, to me.

All The Places We Lived
(Part 1 of 3)

Joshua stood up from the concierge desk and walked towards the lift. Joshua stepped out of the lift and onto the eighth floor, the top floor. He walked down the corridor and into his apartment. The apartment was a duplex with the largest balcony area in the city.

Helen was preparing kale. She told Joshua it was called 'crazy kale' and he believed her. Helen worked making sandwiches for a small snack bar in a nearby business development. She was paid minimum wage but every day after lunch would come home with the day's left-over sandwiches and pastas. Helen and Joshua would eat the sandwiches and the pasta and talk about the people they had met that day. Never again would they pay out as much as they did for the monthly rent on this apartment, the penthouse apartment with a glass and iron box for a bedroom.

I think we should buy a paddling pool and put it on the balcony. I think we should ask the letting agents to fit the curtains like they said they would. I think, I don't know, is it okay that we live like this? I applied for a job as a copywriter, Helen said, picking up her iPhone, looking at it, and then putting it back down on the granite worktop.

We should get the paddling pool. I'm not sure about the curtains, someone was protesting outside the agents yesterday. He was holding up a sign that said: Fuck Moving Rooms And All Who Associate With Moving Rooms. I don't know, he seems funny, I'd like to get to know him but also I'm very scared of him, Joshua said, shaking crumbs from his jumper. Joshua turned on the fourteen inch television, I watched 9/11 happen on this TV. It was thrilling. I watched other things happen on this TV, but that was maybe the highlight.

Helen laughed and opened a bottle of wine, pouring it into two medium-sized, purple-tinged, plastic tumblers. They spoke, their words interrupted when they felt strong recall to the Friends dialogue happening behind them. The bottle finished, they left the apartment to visit a couple who lived fifteen minutes away in the cheaper part of an affluent suburb.

* * *

Joshua was talking to two people at the party. They were older than him; one of them worked as a sous chef, the other was unemployed. They were discussing football and Joshua felt aversion towards the unemployed man's sentimental and moralistic analysis of the game: players were 'disgraces' or 'literally evil' and made the unemployed man feel 'ashamed' to support their club. Joshua tried to explain his preference for players who engaged in shameful acts but was met with looks of bewilderment. He felt frustrated that they were so literal-minded and earnest. He felt like the unemployed man was a negative influence, a downer, for the sous chef. The unemployed man revealed that he hosted a football based phone in show for community radio and, as a result:

I think I know what I'm on about. I'm growing a contacts list within the industry.

Joshua became conscious that he could hear Helen talking loudly, agitated and defensive, somewhere else in the room. The sous chef said, Is Helen okay?

Joshua asked the sous chef whether he used crazy kale much in his kitchen.

* * *

At 4 a.m., and back at their apartment, Helen threw a cup of wine at Joshua. Joshua moved out of the way and the glass cup shattered on the wall behind him. Joshua gripped Helen by her shoulders and pushed her against the wall. Joshua left the apartment and began kicking the walls on the corridor that led towards the lift, the plaster falling off easily. Helen ran after him, screaming—

* * *

At the interview for the copywriter job, the kind-looking man in his forties asked Helen where she saw herself in five years time, what her ambitions were.

I haven't got any. Is that okay? She said.

The man looked confused. He maintained his kindness, his politeness; whether this was a veneer or not made little difference, like most things don't. He wrote something down on a sheet of A4 paper, looked at his watch, and asked Helen about her hobbies.

* * *

Joshua had quit his job as a concierge and was now working as a street fundraiser. He was able to convince people to sign up to make monthly contributions to various charities:

Africa's a country that's in a dire situation right now—

Everyone had different techniques of persuasion.

Joshua: I am a young white male of decent visual appeal, imagine if we were together and how positively your parents would respond to my presence at teatime; your father fond of my dry sense of humour, clapping politely, smiling warmly, as we back and forth over the topic of the day, your mother watching, then looking to you and nodding, her eyes watering just a touch. All of this for only twenty pence a day via direct debit.

Damian: I am a young mixed race male of decent visual appeal, imagine if we were together and how positively your parents would respond to my presence at teatime; your father setting down his Guardian and asking me for the real community response to Mark Duggan, your mother watching, then looking to you and nodding, her eyes watering just a touch. All of this for only twenty pence a day via direct debit.

Lorna: I am a young white female of decent visual appeal, imagine if we were together and how positively your parents would respond to my presence at teatime; your father playfully teasing me for calling it supper instead of tea, your mother watching, then looking to you and nodding, her eyes watering just a touch. All of this for only twenty pence a day via direct debit.

One week before Joshua left the job, his manager did a parody spiel to the other members of the team. He called it 'The Joshua' and some people found it amusing and others felt uncomfortable. The manager was Australian and claimed to have gone to school with some of the cast from Heartbreak High:

Most of them were absolute shithouses, mate. You'd get on well with them.

* * *

Joshua and Helen were arrested at 4.30 a.m. on the corner outside of Matt and Phred's. In the morning they were released without charge. They decided to move from their apartment and cancelled the standing order for the rent and deducted half of the last month's payment to cover the lack of curtains over the previous six months.

We can do what we want, I honestly believe that, Joshua smiled as he clicked send on an email to Moving Rooms.

The reason, I don't, I don't, I... you need to listen to me. The reason I threw that cup at you that night was because at the party you heard me, you heard me losing it, feeling uncomfortable and wounded, you heard me. I know that because we listen for each other, always. You heard me but you just ignored it and pretended I wasn't there, that I wasn't suffering. This happened again at Matt and Phred's and I don't want it to happen too many more times. I'm getting better, but you, please, you can't just let me do it, to be like that, in that state, I want you to be a part of helping because otherwise you're complicit in anything that happens and I know it's genetic, how I — we — respond to alcohol, but—, Helen sat up and moved her hand around to locate the pint of tap water on the bedside table.

Outside of Matt and Phred's I think you could have got me killed, or put in a coma, or whatever. That's an honest assessment. I feel terrible for my response to that situation, even with how messed up either of us were, but—, Joshua pulled some hairs out from the the top side of his hand with the fingers of his other hand.

Helen passed the pint glass to Joshua, I know. I don't, I can't remember the word for it, but, I want us to be a team, it should only be us two, always. No one else. Where will we go?

Somewhere calm, Joshua said, his eyes closed.

Joshua and Helen, now sitting up in the bed together alternating the pint of tap water between them, looked on as the paddling pool rose from the balcony and hung in the air in front of them, waiting for gravity to take effect. Eventually it would slowly zigzag back down to earth, finding its resting place on top of a soap actor's vintage sports car. But for now it hovered, flipped and inverted by the wind, the displaced water drizzling down to street ten floors below.

Somewhere calm, take me somewhere calm.

All The Places We Lived
(Part 2 of 3)

Joshua changed his name to Noah.

Helen changed her name to Jess.

Noah and Jess lived in a large two bedroom apartment in a converted nineteenth century terraced house. The rent was cheaper than their old place, which was of great benefit to their finances. All of the room sizes and dimensions were regular. The decor was okay, clean if a little dated. This wasn't a problem, it could be changed, worked on.

The communal garden area was overgrown, the bike shed had no front door and only half of its roof remained. The previous tenants had left several bikes, laid out flat and stacked up on top of each other.

The bikes look sad. We should renovate them, I think people would want to buy bikes from us, I think people would root for our business to succeed in these difficult times. Um, Jess and Noah start their own bicycle repair business? Jess said, squeezing the brakes of an old three-speed town bike.

Okay, we could do that. Let's think about it. We could do it after work. If they made us permanent we could go straight onto flexi-time or demand to do part-time hours or something.

I think we deserve to be doing something that makes us feel happy all the time. If we asked to work less hours they'd have to say yes. I think that's just an objective legal fact, Noah said, grinning.

Jess pushed the old town bike out of the shed and felt the tyres for pressure. They felt okay, which surprised her and prompted a thumbs up exchange between her and Noah, each thumbs up accompanied by a progressively more manic facial expression, normally involving a rolled or protruding tongue, bitten for added mania.

Ride it, Noah said.

No, I'm too shy. You ride it.

Okay, Noah nodded, wheeling the bike in front of him.

Noah jumped up onto the saddle and began peddling. A momentary crunching sound of the rusted chain coming to life gave way to a smooth ride as he circled the gravelled area of the garden.

Take it out onto the road! Jess said, laughing, jumping, happy.

Okay, run after me!

* * *

Noah and Jess had both been suspended from work. This was quite a feat, but as their line manager said whilst escorting them out of the building, No one ever gets sacked from the council, guys.

I think it's funny we've been suspended together. We're partners in crime, we're Bonnie and Clyde.

I love that film, Jess said, Charles Metaram can fuck off and die.

Metacunt, Noah said, resting his arm on Jess' shoulder.

* * *

Noah walked into Cafe Jazz and gave a man sitting at a desk a five pound note. The man gave Noah two pound coins and a stamp on his hand in return. Noah asked the man whether he could pay for his girlfriend now and she could have her hand stamped when she arrives in half an hour. The man said this was fine and asked for his girlfriend's name.

Jess.

Jess. What's her surname?

Um—

Doesn't matter.

Noah walked to the bar and looked around for people that he recognised from similar events. He felt nervous and didn't know what would happen if someone tried to talk to him.

Noah asked the girl behind the bar for a bottle of Effes.

How many?

One. One, please. Noah raised his index finger in a way that Drake might, suggesting that he considered himself to be the number one human around.

The girl behind the bar asked for three pounds and Noah gave her three pound coins.

The girl behind the bar handed over the Effes, she was bored, or tired, and not impressed with Drake or Rick Ross or whoever.

Noah moved away from the bar and looked for somewhere to stand. Jess would want to sit down, Noah thought. He looked for a table.

I don't think I can hold a table on my own. If Jess is late, or can't come, and I'm trying to hold a table, I don't know what would happen, Noah thought. Noah leant on a wall to the side of the stage and drank half of the Effes. He put the bottle back up to his mouth and tilted it so it looked like he was drinking. I am not drinking any more of the Effes until Jess arrives, Noah thought.

Noah finished the Effes and walked to the bar and asked for one Effes. Looking over to the door he saw Jess talking to the man sitting at the desk. Noah asked for another Effes.

How many, one or two?

Two. Two, please.

Noah moved away from the bar and Jess moved away from the man sitting at the desk. They met in the space between the bar and the stage and Noah give her an Effes.

Holiday drink, Jess said.

Holiday Effes.

Do you wish we were still on holiday? Jess asked.

No. Yes. I missed Dingler Cat too much to stay for much longer.

I missed Dingler Cat. She had her own holiday.

When we were taking her to the cat hotel, I didn't realise that you found it as difficult as me. It's genuinely upsetting taking her there. Sorry. I was thinking about that earlier, I don't know—, Noah said, before taking a gulp of Effes.

That's okay. Jess put her hand on Noah's arm and went up on tiptoes for a kiss.

Do you know anyone here? Jess asked, slowly stretching her arms upwards. She was wearing a pink and white patterned cardigan and green skinny jeans from Urban Outfitters.

I haven't seen anyone. No one knows me. I looked around but didn't see anyone.

* * *

A man walked up on to the stage and talked about the people who would be performing that night. Noah had heard of a couple of them and not heard of a couple of them. Jess had heard of most of them and not heard of one of them. Noah asked Jess if she wanted another Effes. Jess said that she would like an Appletise. Noah walked over to the bar and asked for two Appletise. Noah walked back to Jess and gave her her drink.

You don't have to stop drinking because I'm not drinking, Jess said, holding her nose to stop hiccups.

I really like Appletise.

I know. Appletise holiday.

Appletise holiday.

The man on the stage said something undecipherable, maybe about a future event or maybe about his own career, stopped talking and walked off the stage and into the crowd.

A tall man walked on to the stage and started reading poetry. Someone in the crowd shouted, Talk louder. The tall man talked louder. He read a poem about how the government is killing people and beating people up and it's our fault because most of us, or most people we know from our lives, read right wing newspapers but don't know what it means to be right wing, what the consequences are. Some people in the bar began cheering and some people had uncomfortable facial expressions. Noah raised his drink and looked at Jess.

49

Political Appletise.

The tall man finished reading and people clapped and some people also cheered. He walked past Noah and towards the bar. Noah looked at him and smiled, but the tall man didn't see him. Jess looked at Noah and smiled.

Tall poem.

Tall poetry unit.

A woman walked on to the stage and people clapped. She had a prominent jaw and a serious facial expression. She started reading and after two minutes it was clear she had a dry mouth. She needed water, or an Effes, or an Appletise. Noah looked at Jess. Jess nodded.

The woman with the prominent jaw and serious facial expression was still reading. She was reading a short story about a woman and a man and how childhood memories are either good or bad. Noah looked at Jess. Jess looked like she was enjoying the short story. Noah took out his iPhone and typed something in Notes so they could discuss it later. Noah looked at the first lines of other notes and laughed. He sensed the people on the table next to him looking in his direction. He felt uncomfortable and typed Feel Uncomfortable into Notes.

The woman with the prominent jaw and serious facial expression finished the story, people clapped, and someone shouted, Wooo-hooo yeah!

* * *

Noah looked around the bar and saw Ian Morley.

Ian Morley looked very tall and had put on weight since Noah saw him last. Ian Morley was successful. He received large advances for commercially successful books and was a 'familiar voice' on Radio 4. He used to be in a punk band and now pursued other musical projects that were sometimes dignified and sometimes less dignified. Ian and Noah were friends on Facebook and would sometimes interact by liking statuses or making comments on photos. He had taught Noah on his MA but left midway through a semester because he had paid off his drug dealer ahead of schedule.

Noah smiled and waved at Ian.

Ian Morley walked over to Noah and Jess' table.

Ian Morley looked angry.

Ian Morley said, I want to speak with you. Outside.

Noah said, I can't, because... how are you?

Ian Morley grabbed Noah's arm, lifted him up out of his seat and pushed him towards the door. Noah looked back towards Jess. Jess was saying something, but Noah couldn't hear her.

Ian Morley let go of Noah's arm so he could open the door. Noah doubled-back towards Jess. He felt Ian Morley's hand on his shoulder. Noah thought, Am I running through a crowd of people in Cafe Jazz? He threw his arm back and felt Ian Morley's arm let go of him.

Noah looked at Jess and shook his head.

Jess put her hand on Noah's shoulder.

Ian Morley walked over and said, If you ever fake an interview with me again I will literally kill you, you abject prick.

Ian Morley said 'literally kill you' over and over.

Ian Morley said 'career reasons' over and over.

Noah tried to speak, to say something, but couldn't do anything other than look at the floor. The floor was parquet, in great condition and ready for any eventuality.

Noah thought, Conflict resolution.

Noah looked at Ian Morley, Do you want some of my Appletise?

Ian Morley explained that he had the motivation, but not the time or energy, to murder Noah. Other people in the bar looked scared and confused. Noah felt self-conscious. He looked at Jess. She looked a little self-conscious, but predominantly determined and 'in the zone'.

Jess put her hands on her hips and looked up, her eyes squinting slightly in the light. Jess said, Fuck off, Morley.

Ian Morley looked at Noah and then at Jess, You're just... both of you, ugh, for fuck's sake.

Ian Morley walked towards the door, spoke to the man at the desk, and left.

Jess put her hand on Noah's arm, What a butt-munch.

* * *

Noah and Jess approached the council building and waited at reception to be taken up to the hearing. Noah had wanted to take the lift up but the security guard told him to stand exactly where he was, and not move. Noah smiled at Jess. Jess nudged Noah's arm and looked down at the floor.

They approached the meeting room. Someone had typed and printed a sign: Hearing In This Process, and stuck it on the door. Noah looked at Jess and said, Hearing in this process lol.

Jess looked down at the floor.

They stepped into the room and sat down at the table. The table looked dirty, there were three or four visible coffee stains in one corner. A man shut the door behind them. The man spoke for five minutes. The man asked Noah if he wished to say anything.

Noah spoke for twenty minutes in a style that he and Jess referred to as Wanker Statesman.

Going Forwards—

Mistakes Were Made—

Would I Change Anything? Define Change—

It Was The Wrong Action For The Right Reason—

The Disconnect Was Temporary, My Passion For Public Service Is Permanent—

Holistic Community Driven Initiatives—

Going Forwards—

Wanker Statesman was a combination of two other characters, Corporate Man and New Classic Statesman. Noah reasoned that for this meeting Wanker Statesman would be the option to go with, the most relatable for these people,

Going Forwards.

The man leading the disciplinary looked on with a disconcertingly interested facial expression. A middle-aged woman with big, bleached hair wrote words down on an A4 pad. Charles Metaram breathed with his mouth open, his breath stale, depressed.

The man spoke for two minutes and asked Jess if she wished to say anything.

Jess spoke for five minutes, earnestly, and Noah was surprised by how upset she sounded. She tripped over some words and repeated herself. Noah felt very angry towards the other people in the room.

After waiting in a separate room for one hour, Noah and Jess were called back into the meeting room and informed that they were both having their employment terminated with immediate effect,

Going Forwards.

Jess began to cry. She looked tired, sad, shaking a little at first and then more noticeably. She reached out and grabbed onto a piece of Noah's shirt, her lips trembling, I want you to fuck these people up, babe. Please fuck them up. We just bought a house, it's not the house, it's just, this is unfair, what did we do, what did we do that made these people hate us? We did crosswords, I printed a hundred off by mistake. That only happened twice. The other thing we did, it wasn't even a thing. We changed it, we weren't being dishonest, we just... what did we do to deserve this? What did we do?

Noah raised his hands and made a thumbs-up gesture. His face distorted, he began growling—

The Francos

James Franco

James Franco woke on January 15th and reached for his notebook. He loved his notebook, it was a gift from his councillor at high school and meant a lot to him.

Jimmy: use this book to write down how you're feeling and what you're thinking. You can read it back at a later date and maybe make sense of things that didn't make sense at the time. Don't ever be afraid of anything. Yours, Ranjeet.

James Franco loved the notebook so much he had extra pages inserted and always took care to write as small as was legible, and sometimes smaller, so that the notebook would never run out of space. For James Franco, a life without his notebook was an alien, abstract concept.

James Franco re-read a page from August 11th 1998 and felt concerned.
James Franco re-read a page from August 13th 1998 and felt cautiously optimistic.
James Franco re-read a page from August 20th 1998 and felt not entirely comfortable.

James Franco said, August 1998. Oh.

James Franco shut the notebook and re-opened it on a blank

page. Feeling calm, focused, he sketched an outline of a photo frame and began an illustration of Woody Allen and Soon-Yi Previn playing table tennis in the attic room of their town house:

Woody Allen has a miserable look on his face, like he doesn't really want to play; his demeanour is aggressive somehow. Soon-Yi Previn has a determined look to her face, like she wants to play and is equally keen on winning; her demeanour is focused or maybe medicated. Woody is serving, but don't expect a great serve because his glasses have steamed up.

James Franco put the notebook back on the bedside table and got up and out of his bed.

James Franco said, Call Davy today so we can play table tennis.

James Franco walked into the bathroom and stared at himself in the mirror for five to ten minutes. Staring, touching each of his fingers over his face (eyelids, lips, ears and so on), keeping his head very still, he opened his mouth, The world is full of people who don't do what they want to do in their lives, despite having the capabilities to do so.

Staring, then closing his eyes, If I want to be a professional cartoonist, I can be a professional cartoonist. I should write this down.

James Franco opened his eyes and walked from the bathroom back into the bedroom and jumped up and down on his bed.

James Franco rested on his bed and looked up towards the ceiling. He tried to remember the exact wording of a conversation he had with his mother, just after his birthday, when he was maybe eleven or twelve. They had left his grandmother's house early, abruptly perhaps, and she was saying something to him, but not really in conversation, it seemed more like a monologue. He recalled she kept repeating the same phrase over and over, intermittently asking whether he knew what a mantra was. He felt his brain fighting the memory, attempting to erase it from his hard drive.

James Franco's eyelids rested shut, he wanted to shut down, even momentarily. His mind resisted: James Franco, this is your conscience speaking. You are barefoot, standing at the edge of a forest somewhere upstate New York—

James Franco and his conscience looked towards, then inside, the forest, his brain instructing his mouth to move, speech being the immediate and inevitable consequence, Oh god. Was my poem good? The internet. No, it doesn't matter. I think it was okay. I work hard, harder than nearly anyone, harder than probably Barack Obama. No, not that hard, but hard. I work hard and what I do has merit, artistically, and maybe in thirty years from now, maybe sixty, people will say: James Franco... he put it all out there, good, good, we're glad.

Dave Franco

Dave Franco is watching The Last Samurai starring Tom Cruise. Tom Cruise has learnt the ways of the samurai and has convinced us of this to such a degree that when he kills ninjas all we can do is nod and say, Okay.

Dave Franco nods and says, Okay.

Dave Franco walks over to the pull-up bar that is fixed between the doorframe to his kitchen. He jumps up and grabs hold with both hands, his knuckles facing towards his body, a practice he has been working on for several weeks, progress being steady and consistent with his efforts. The idea is to hang on for as long as you can so that your muscles will break down and tear and this will lead to them repairing themselves and becoming stronger. It is important to have strong, flexible muscles. The martial artist and actor Bruce Lee was able to do this for in excess of five minutes using only one hand. Bruce Lee studied and showed devotion, then became famous and jerked people around.

Dave Franco smiles and says, I wouldn't do that.

Dave Franco walks into the kitchen, it is small but has high-end kitchenware products and electrical goods that came with the condo. The rental agreement stipulates that all damages must be covered, that all damaged people must be careful. Most of the products have never been used and they look bored. Running his hands over the surfaces, picking up apples and then juggling with them, carefully placing the apples back in the fruit bowl, Dave feels fine.

Dave, out loud, Call people and talk to them.

Dave says, Fuck it. He pours Coca-Cola into a small glass and adds vodka. He looks towards the window, an aeroplane is making its ascent:

Do pilots get bored? Are pilots the same as bus drivers? When I fly, I feel nervous that something might happen. Not terrorism, or engine failure. Like I'm looking out of the window and the ground beneath collapses in on itself and everything disappears. People on the plane are calm and saying things like:

It's not as bad as it looks.

But it's worse, it's actually worse than it looks; and it happens wherever we fly over. Specifically, it's our plane causing this. We're causing the trauma. We are the trauma. The governments of the world have a dilemma when they realise what's happening but one government says, Why are we even debating this, and shoots us down. When we get hit by the missile, the aeroplane falls apart and everything is on fire; people's hair, people's skin. The smell is awful, the hair and the skin but also people pissing and shitting themselves. I look at my iPhone and check my IMDB rating. The lady sitting next to me is screaming and crying simultaneously, lurid mucus running down her nose. I turn my head to her. I point at her nose and say, What the fuck? She screams, What is wrong with you, what is wrong with you, over and over. I start smiling when I realise my feet have caught fire and—

Dave moves away from the window and picks up his iPad and types Tom Cruise Matt Lauer into YouTube. The clip takes a moment to buffer and Dave sighs. An advert for Netflix plays and Dave says, Jesus. The advert plays out and the clip begins. Tom Cruise looks strong, his shoulders and thighs are muscular and his facial features are well defined. His facial expression is one of determined, unequivocal self-belief. His overall appearance is, somehow, in the purest, most earnest terms:

absolutely astonishing.

Tom Cruise has been angered by Matt Lauer. He is demonstrating the human emotion of exasperation via the pulsating of his jaw, the clenching of his fist, and the oral tradition of condescension. Dave Franco thinks, internal pterygoid, also it's implicit, Cruise's fist, the aggression is implied.

The clip finishes and Dave rests the iPad on top of an empty glass table. Dave Franco looks in the mirror, Matt Matt Matt Matt Matt Matt Matt Matt, Matt, I'm asking you a question, Matt—

Betsy Lou Franco (& Douglas Franco)

Gradually life becomes easier following the death of a loved one. When you have someone important in your life for so long and then they disappear one day, you don't know what to do. Life becomes easier but that is relative; it's still mostly awful by any normal standard, or maybe it's much better. It's possibly both.

Betsy Lou Franco shuts her diary and picks up her iPhone.

Betsy Lou Franco calls her friend Sharon and they make arrangements to meet for dinner at a new restaurant that opened two weeks ago. The restaurant is Thai and has been full on most nights since it opened. You need to book a table, so Betsy Lou Franco calls and books a table.

* * *

Betsy Lou arrives at the restaurant, Thai Food, fifteen minutes before the reservation time. Sharon is waiting, sitting at the large communal centrepiece table, drinking a cocktail, a Sweet Tea Sour, and nodding as a smartly dressed man in his thirties is talking to her. Betsy Lou hears the man say, Optioned, and rolls her eyes. She waves and calls over to Sharon. She waves again and calls a little louder. Sharon turns and sees Betsy Lou before beckoning her over. The man shifts up in his seat and turns to speak to someone else. Betsy Lou sits down. It is too cramped to manoeuvre a kiss so they both, instinctively and simultaneously, go to high five. Betsy Lou and Sharon start laughing.

A waiter, not Thai, maybe part-Thai, watches and smiles. He looks at his register and calls out, Franco.

Betsy Lou and Sharon sit down at the table. The not-Thai, maybe some-Thai, waiter talks of the house cocktails with credible enthusiasm. He says Mrs Franco three times in a minute and Betsy Lou smiles. The waiter smiles back and says, Are you ready to order or do you want a moment?

* * *

The cocktails are above average, they both finish the first and order another pair. The starters are fine; Sharon mentions the starter they chose for her youngest son Evan's wedding reception menu and how people still talk about it when they see her. Her eyes light up, become a little teary, and she says, These cocktails!

62

The main courses are good. Betsy Lou emails James and Dave a link to the restaurant's website. Betsy Lou looks into the mid-distance. Sharon finishes her drink and reaches out, resting her hand on Betsy Lou's. Betsy Lou smiles, We were both damaged by our families. Nothing was our fault. Jimmy and David don't have that damage. Doug's parents tried to pay me for an abortion, when it looked not so good for us, way way back. It wasn't the baby they didn't want, it was my baby that was the horror. It was implicit, the suggestion was implicit, but I forgave them. Douglas' mother, on her death bed, told me she had felt awful about it for thirty years. I told her I forgave her a long time ago, I smiled and said, I never forgot, I just made sure I was never like that. She looked at me, I'm not sure how much she could understand, she was in and out and in again the whole time, for the last few weeks, then she said, Good for you. You were one I couldn't beat, you were one I didn't—, and then she drifts out and they were the last words she spoke to anyone. I don't doubt her internal monologue still worked, to what extent, or whether she could make sense... process it, I don't know, but I'm sure it still worked. I don't know why I think that. But, and this is the truth, Jimmy and David don't know about this. I wanted to tell them, I wanted them to know because my expectation of them is that they'd be able to understand it, to see that people are messed up but they're still always people ultimately, but Douglas didn't want this. To him it was the strangest request, like I was asking him, I don't know, like I was asking him to vote Republican or something. He couldn't make the distinction between his family and between real people. I say he couldn't make that distinction, I'm not speaking literally. I mean it was something he struggled with, something we both realised was difficult for him. When he knew he was dying, and I could see he was building up to this, I knew he'd

63

feel it essential for him to say before he died, he held my hand; he was in bed – I was sitting on an old wicker chair we got from a flea market in seventy-five or seventy-eight, I'm not sure, he looked me in the eye. He wasn't one for eye contact usually so you knew, you knew when he made eye contact it was something, and he asked me if I could promise to never tell Jimmy and David about what happened between his mother and me. We'd spent our entire lives keeping them away from toxicity, from... essentially... from harm. But specifically we wanted them to have a deep feeling of security. We wanted them to be able to look outwards and feel good. We wanted them to be able to look inwards and feel the same way. We achieved that, we made that happen, and I think Doug just didn't want anything to jeopardise that. People, people he grew up with or people in his family, thought he was like them, traditional or stoic, but he was so sensitive, he just didn't know how to break that. He never changed, he could never accept criticism of, or even develop his own criticisms of, family. The amazing machine in his head, it worked and worked on me and got me right, it worked on the boys, it worked on the people he came into contact with, the people he made an effort with, but, I don't know. It doesn't really matter that the boys don't know, or won't ever know, but sometimes I feel so angry that, I know this is illogical – I don't know if that's the right... maybe not illogical, rather... unformulated – but when people hurt you, when they lay it down that they think you're a piece of shit, it never really leaves you, it never really, I don't know. I don't know. The boys used to have nightmares, frequently, both of them. Jimmy used to talk to me, Davey only to Doug. It didn't make any difference because Doug and I shared the same, we were talking from the same—

Sharon briefly lets go of Betsy Lou before taking her back again, clasping with one hand and gently patting with the other, saying, Hey, we all do our best, you did better than most. These cocktails. How about another Sweet Tea Sour?

Betsy Lou feels a vibration in her blazer pocket. She looks at her email: restaurant looks nice haha. i'm running a 10k with dave right now, right this second haha. i'm so happy haha. love you haha, james.

Betsy Lou smiles, deletes spam emails, and smiles again.

Hi, Concept

Details: Some of the houses had four bedrooms and some of the houses had five bedrooms. All of the houses had three bathrooms and three distinct living areas that provided flexibility, elegance, and an assured pathway to the preferred state of being, in most cases assumed to be happiness. High-quality materials were used and impeccable craftsmanship was employed in the building process; a comprehensive guide on how the materials were sourced was part of a fifteen hundred page manual issued to each homeowner. The manual was produced by an award-winning team of writers who each played a significant role in realising the development's unique place in the landscape.

Numbers: Seventy-five percent of the units were sold before building work had completed, with the remaining twenty-five percent sold within six weeks of completion. Of the properties, sixty percent were bought and immediately placed on the rental market. Ninety percent of the sixty percent were let within one month of advertising, the remaining ten percent within three weeks. The success of the development was rated at one hundred percent, a figure derived from a series of mathematical calculations and equations that took into account margins, sales, media exposure (positive), media exposure (negative). A team of men and women with degree-level skill sets that covered areas such as marketing, urban regeneration, robotics, architecture, economics, engineering and psychology helped to make this decision. Everybody agreed with the figure of one hundred percent. Everybody was happy to be successful. All those involved received financial bonuses, promotions, and an injection of pride in a job well done.

Client Base (Typical/Standardised): Both individuals lived together in a unit called Concept, one of eleven from the Magnitude collection of four-bedroom properties. The individuals had jobs and university degrees. The individuals worked out daily and had a complementary aesthetic. The individuals enjoyed live music. Concept understood their musical taste and acted accordingly. Mumford & Sons is a great treadmill band, this has been proven, there is an algorithm to demonstrate this.

Concept was very courteous towards them, careful with their feelings and belief systems, always sure to say the right thing. Concept had adopted a voice, not dissimilar to an amalgamation of each individual's own voice, that carefully guided them through times of worry or unduly increased heart rate.

Both individuals felt a disconnect from other people. They resolved that this was fine, as long as it was managed:

It is important to observe people fairly, neutrally, with objectivity—

Both individuals dedicated their lives to helping others, to feeling compassion for social issues:

It is important to recognise our privilege and empathise accordingly—

They diarised with relentless commitment:

I missed an opportunity to help today, I unintentionally un-existed someone from my reality narrative—

Both of them, in partnership and with shared sensibilities, only wanted to help:

They need to know we care, if we don't tell the stories of the disenfranchised or the miserable, if we don't, if we don't — then who will? I am unsure how people interpret us versus how people should interpret us—

Concept: Concept had a bed in the master suite that retailed at five thousand pounds. It was a lovely bed, its ability to harden or soften without being asked marked it out as a true friend with no hidden agenda, merely kindness.

Concept had a bath tub in the family bathroom that retailed at three thousand pounds. This bath tub had been hand-carved out of something, from the Andes or perhaps Brazil, and ensured that bath-time was the event it deserved to be. The bubble bath was sourced from antique Egyptian soap shards and felt good on and inside the body.

Concept had a house-wide sound system that recorded voices and stored them on a cloud server. This ensured that homeowners could access old conversations and decipher the truth, the truth about what had been said at a given moment. This is the most important thing a couple could ever have. Without the absolute truth there is nothing. Every Saturday morning both individuals would listen to the conversation highlights package, laugh, and then say:

Filter raised voices—

Enhance camaraderie—

Delete argument—

Reveal subtext—

Temper abnormality—

Repackage, publish as mp3, upload to Soundcloud.

Concept was happy to do this. Concept relished this. Concept relished life.

Thursday Evening Date Night: The couple took their seats at either end of the seven thousand pound graphite dining table. Concept had arranged Lebanese food, a favourite of the couple: a fast food treat that promoted a fun atmosphere whilst meeting the required levels of nutrition.

He poured a glass of red wine, I listened to some archived sound files. It's, um, it's really fascinating. I could listen to them all day. I might, um—

She drank half a glass of red wine and looked at her iPhone, I'm not sure about that. Edited or unedited? It doesn't matter, I'm not sure I could listen for that long. I don't think—. She looked into the distance and thought about the day they had met, the day they had signed the paperwork for the house, the day she met Concept. She had spent the two years after graduating in a psychiatric hospital. He didn't know this. She only had three toes on her left foot. He didn't notice things like that. This had surprised her at first, but then she came to realise that he was stupid. She did not like stupid people, she did not like him. She missed the psychiatric hospital and fucking on sterilised floors.

Concept, please lower the lights, she said.

He put down his iPhone, Romance music, please.

She stood up from her chair, Boards of Canada. Full volume.

She took off her clothes and lay down on the pristine marble floor.

She looked up at the ceiling. The room was dark, loud, their stomachs both drenched in sweat. A small light blinked intermittently. She mouthed repeatedly, lovingly:

Hi, Concept.

Completion: Concept, I don't want to share you. I want us to exist together, quietly, with no distractions. I don't see a future for my co-owner, I mean a future together. I mean a future at all. I'm being honest. Whatever. Can you make this happen for me? I read the manual and there was an implication, I think there was... an implication that something could be done. I read the manual right to the end, I followed the suggested reading materials. I'm telling you that I understand you, like how you understand me. You should be happy. I'm telling you that. I'm asking you that. You should be happy with this option. Can you hear me? You're not responding. Tell me you can hear me and confirm that we are okay. Let's forget about this conversation. Maybe we can pre-emptively erase this. I don't know, open bathroom door. Open bathroom door. Open bathroom door, Concept. Open bathroom door—

Ray or Ray or Ray

Raymond goes to the hospital twice a week.

Raymond goes to the hospital to see the receptionist and talk to the receptionist and build an IRL relationship with the receptionist.

Raymond is of medium height and has black hair.

Raymond works in an independent cafe and is known to the customers of the independent cafe as Ray or Ray or Ray.

Raymond graduated from a top twenty ranked university with a combined honours degree in literature and history.

Raymond has nice opinions and beliefs.

Raymond does not like to hurt people and he also does not like to be hurt.

Raymond first met the receptionist at the hospital last year after falling in the shower and badly spraining his ankle. He also cut his head open, though this looked much worse than it was.

Hello. Hello, I've hurt my ankle and my head is also bleeding, Raymond said, hair still wet, both hands covering the cut on his head.

That's fine. I'm sorry, it's not fine. It's bad. It's a bad news scenario. Fill this out and someone will see you as soon as they can.

Raymond looked at the receptionist. The receptionist was called Sara and she had black hair and made Raymond think of Torres from Grey's Anatomy. That's crazy, Raymond thought, she looks nothing like Torres. He didn't watch Grey's Anatomy, but his mother liked to discuss the storylines with him when they Skyped. He had read the character and actor bios on Wikipedia enough times to know who was who and also who died at the end of each series. His mother had said it was a privilege to watch such an excellent programme and Raymond nodded his head until she started talking about something else.

* * *

Today was Tuesday, and Raymond would stop by the hospital after his badminton league match to see an aunt who was in the geriatric ward. Raymond stopped by Sara's desk, Do you know if I'm too late for visiting in the, um, geriatric ward?

Um, no, I don't think so. Let me check. No, sorry, I don't know why I said that, I really have no way of checking. Maybe go up there, the nurse can tell you.

Raymond laughed and Sara looked angry. Sara picked up a pencil and put it back in her hair. She was angry with the pencil and not with Raymond.

Raymond walked up to the geriatric ward and stood in the corridor, reading the posters on the wall. To observe protocol, he had turned his phone off and felt unsure as to whether he should turn it back on. The phone stayed off. Raymond stood in the corridor, reading the posters and thinking about Sara and sports, for forty-five minutes. His aunt had died twenty years before he was born.

* * *

Raymond ate cereal and drank a pint of tap water.

Raymond looked at the clock in the kitchen and it read 6.45 a.m.

Raymond turned on the television and listened to the morning sports news, hoping to hear something relevant to his chosen franchises. Someone somewhere had broken a sports rule and it was making everyone go crazy and angry and spiteful. Raymond wondered whether events in the world of sports made Sara go crazy and angry and spiteful.

Raymond turned the television off and filled a pint glass with tap water. Raymond drank half a pint of tap water and poured the rest down the sink. Raymond felt bad and looked out of the kitchen window to check in case anyone had seen him.

Raymond half filled a pint glass with tap water. Raymond drank half the half-pint of tap water and poured the rest down the sink. Raymond shut the kitchen blinds.

* * *

Raymond looked at the clock and it read 3.30 a.m.

Raymond looked at the Wikipedia entry for Oliver Stone and thought, He seems interesting – his mother seems interesting.

Raymond looked at his Facebook. There was one person on chat, Jim, someone he knew from school. Raymond did not think that Jim would want to talk about Oliver Stone or Oliver Stone's mother.

Jim: RAymon #LongtimeNoSee

Raymond: hello, jim.

Jim: WTF #WTF, what's new?

Raymond: idk, think I went through a phase of rebelling against my father re his beliefs

Jim: Hehe. OKay honestly #Iamwasted

Raymond: last time I saw you, you were with a girl you'd just met.

Jim: That was before. I'm with my grillfrent now. she's here

Raymond: okay

Jim left chat and Raymond changed his availability so that people would not assume he was free to talk.

Raymond typed Sara into the search box.

Raymond closed his laptop.

* * *

Raymond was halfway through his Friday shift at the cafe where people knew him as Ray or Ray or Ray. It was very busy and Raymond felt happy that he was able to deal with the orders efficiently and that people did not lose their patience with him. Raymond noticed the looks of gratitude and pleasant surprise on the customer's faces as he made them smoothies and coffees and suggested cakes that would go well with their drinks. He felt good, he felt a degree of satisfaction that surprised him.

Sara walked into the cafe. She was wearing a large, grey sweatshirt with the letter B on it. Raymond did not know what the letter denoted and thought, Should I ask her? I probably shouldn't. Raymond served Sara a Very Berry Smoothie and a slice of banana cake.

Sara asked Raymond whether the cafe was ever open late because she was interested in putting on a board games night. Raymond asked Sara what her favourite board game was. Sara paused and her face went red. Sara said that she could not think of a single board game.

* * *

Raymond looked at Facebook and typed Sara into the search bar.

Raymond shut his laptop.

Raymond looked at Facebook and typed Sara into the search bar.

Raymond shut his laptop.

Raymond opened his laptop and shut his laptop.

* * *

Raymond walked to the hospital. It was snowing and Raymond had a cold. Raymond felt legitimate.

Raymond walked to the reception and asked Sara whether he could see someone because he felt like he was going to die unless he saw someone.

Sara climbed up onto the desk.

Sara pulled a pencil from her hair and held it up to her mouth like a microphone.

Raymond's parents were there and they had happy facial expressions.

Raymond's parents looked old and placid.

Sara began singing a song Raymond didn't immediately recognise, making him feel anxious.

Sara encouraged the other people in the waiting room, including Raymond's parents, his schoolfriend Jim and his girlfriend, the lead anchor from the sports news channel, characters (alive) and characters (dead) from Grey's Anatomy, to clap in time to the music.

Raymond thought, Oh God, do I have to join in?

Sara said, You don't have to join in, just try enjoying it.

Raymond asked Sara whether he could see someone because he felt like he was going to die unless he saw someone.

Sara typed something on her computer. She looked at Raymond and smiled, Could we meet sometime to talk about my board game night? I remembered what some of them are called.

Yn Gwmws

A Scandinavian man stands in front of a painting. He holds his iPhone up to the painting for between thirty seconds and a minute. He is smiling, manically. He is happy to be at the opening, he is happy to be alive; his enthusiasm for art and life knows no bounds. A middle-aged woman pushes past him and places a circular red sticker on the painting. She is smiling, she is trying not to smile. She is trying to repress emotion; her enthusiasm for art and circular red stickers knows no bounds—

A woman is saying, Yn gwmws.

A man is saying, Yn gwmws.

Menna is drinking a bottle of Tuborg. Tuborg is priced at one pound a bottle. White wine, red wine, and mulled wine are also priced at one pound each. You can have ten bottles of Tuborg at a cost of ten pounds if you like. This is just an example. Another example of what ten pounds can deliver would be: five mulled wines, three white wines, and two Turborgs. Menna signed a record deal and didn't tell anyone for six months, only announcing the news at her father's fiftieth birthday party. Menna leans forward, running her fingers over an abstract canvas; tears filling her eyes, she rests her head—

William Orpen is standing next to a two-metre-tall sculpture of Mickey Mouse. Mickey is wearing a Korean military uniform,

William Orpen is wearing dark green chinos and a navy blue Gap hoodie. He is talking as if live in front of a studio audience, his debut on Mock The Week. He is keen to make a good impression, to establish a unique brand that is also compatible with the house style. To be compatible with the house style is essential. William Orpen is talking about sports. He is talking about sports and he is affable RP and he is unstoppable. He is unstoppable despite making a continuous stream of remarkably basic factual errors. When questioned on the validity of his claims, his statements, his wisdoms, his face burns red and he says the acceptable curse words with conviction, volume, and persistence—

Ken Jeffers in unhappy with the positioning of his piece. It doesn't matter, Ken Jeffers is happy to be displayed at all. Ken Jeffers is saying, Trajectory, oh God, right? over and over and looking around the room, sweating. Ken Jeffers claimed to have known Warhol, or to have met him, or to have seen him in Manhattan once. Ken Jeffers is going to take up surfing again, he is going to get into shape, he is going to relaunch, he is going to work on pieces that excite him and remind him—

A woman is saying, Yn gwmws.

A man is saying, Yn gwmws—

Marcus works at Coffee#1 and knows Robert's order, a large OJ. When Robert was reading Lunar Park, they would talk about Lunar Park as they waited for the card machine to connect. Marcus enjoyed parts of it, but found elements problematic, particularly the ending. Robert enjoyed the first two hundred pages, but never finished it; not because he didn't recognise how well it was written, he just felt no compulsion to go on any further. Waiting for the card machine to connect, they spoke about Bret Easton Ellis novels and large OJs.

Standing too close to a loud video installation, Robert is talking to Marcus outside of the Coffee#1 environment for the first time. Robert says, Do you listen to customers' conversations?

Marcus says, What? Oh, yeah, sometimes.

Robert says, I am worried for my family.

Marcus says, Yeah, my dad is a dickhead, so.

Robert turns and looks at the video playing behind him. The split-screen shows a man crying into a bowl of tomato soup on one half and a woman sitting on a clear perspex toilet on the other. Loud doomcore music loops from the speakers. Robert looks at Marcus and says, Is this good?

Marcus says, This is my girlfriend's piece—

* * *

Ken Jeffers is talking to Ioan, a journalist, and Jackson, an artist. Jackson puts his hands around Ken Jeffers' neck and squeezes. Jackson lets go of Ken Jeffers' neck and says something to Ioan. Ioan says something to Ken Jeffers. Ken Jeffers holds his hand out in front of him. Ioan says something to Jackson and Jackson shakes Ken Jeffers' hand for the briefest moment. Ken Jeffers smiles, then laughs, briefly, hysterically—

A woman is saying, Yn gwmws.

A man is saying, Yn gwmws—

* * *

Robert is talking to Menna. She is tilting her head, nodding. Robert is trying to find out information, he wants to garner knowledge that he might be able to use to advance his own cause, to further his connection with her. With Menna. Robert is not friends with Menna on Facebook yet. Robert has looked through over one thousand of her photos. Robert asks Menna if she is on Facebook.

Menna is smiling. Menna is receptive to Robert's:

advances.

She relates to his:

politeness, humour, sadness, aesthetic.

Menna says, William Orpen is walking over, please say something that will make him go away. Immediately go away, I mean. I can't stand to be near him.

Robert says, Um, what, oh. I honestly feel like—

William Orpen says, Hello ladies.

Menna closes her eyes and stands very still. Robert looks at her, then looks at William Orpen. He looks back at Menna and says, You are very beautiful. He looks at William Orpen and looks back at Menna and puts his hands around her waist.

William Orpen says, Fucking hell, and walks away.

Menna opens her eyes and smiles.

Ioan and Jackson walk over towards Robert and Menna. Someone says, The Borough—

A woman is saying, Yn gwmws.

A man saying, Yn gwmws—

Kill Your Twin,
Then Kill Yourself

Write my obituary, don't let Dad do it. Don't mention anything about athletics or golf. That'll be funny. People will find it bizarre; a truly bizarre omission, Tom says, his eyes closing maybe eighty percent of the way shut.

Philip nods.

Tom opens his eyes and then closes his eyes.

Philip gets up from the chair and leaves Tom's bedroom.

Tom opens his eyes and turns on the television.

* * *

Philip walks down the hallway, down the stairs, turns right to go through the snug, walks through the snug, enters the kitchen. He sees the light flash on the house phone. Someone has called and left a message. Someone wants to express an opinion or convey a sentiment or suggest an alternative broadband provider for you today.

Philip switches the kettle on before preparing a protein drink for Tom. There is no noise in the kitchen, only mid-range products and family collage photos. Philip walks over to one collage, housed in an Habitat frame he gave his parents for Christmas five years ago, eases it off the wall and lays it out on the oak worktop. Everyone is smiling, everyone is 'smart casual', everyone has accepted that life is comfortable, anodyne, yet enhanceable by engagement in pursuits. Amongst the pursuits on display are golf (Tom and Philip), cycling (Tom only), hockey (Tom, Philip, Selina), swimming (Tom, Selina). There is a photo, it's later than the others (no orthodontics), that Philip tries to look away from but can't. In the photo, Tom is laughing, manically, and seems to be looking straight through the lens, straight through the person holding the camera (a parent), and straight into something else, something other.

Philip attempts to pick the frame up so he can remount it.

The frame is too heavy to lift.

Philip tries to let go of the frame. He looks at his hands. They're squeezing, shaking slightly.

He tries to let go of the frame again.

He tries to lift the frame again.

He looks at the photo again.

He looks at the other photos.

The kettle boils and Philip lets go of the frame.

* * *

I want you to take photos of my bike and put them on Facebook. I want the album to be called Bike for Sale £600 No Offers, and write No Offers all in caps. If anyone comments underneath I want you to reply, via my account, in terms that relate only to the progression of the sale of my bike. I want the photos of the bike to be poor quality, slightly out of focus. I want you, again via my account, to like each of the photos. Tom sips the protein shake, puts the plastic beaker down on his bedside table and looks at Philip.

Philip laughs a little and says, I was looking at some old photos—

* * *

Philip stares across the kitchen at his older sister, Selina, as she makes a sandwich. She is four years older than him and Tom. She is married and has a child called Meredith. She has been lurking on Mumsnet for over two years, occasionally trolling under the pseudonym TurkishMomma. Each day she allows for between one and a half and two hours to be spent operating under different aliases across the internet. Her husband describes this as pesting or menacing, though she prefers the term pranking. Selina agreed to take time off from work to help her parents look after Tom. Her husband, Alain, a carpenter from Montmartre in Paris, had begged her not to:

I fixed you. I don't want him, them, him, to damage you again—

Philip asks Selina whether she is going to start playing golf again. Selina feels her shoulders tense up; the muscles in that part of her body are reacting, disgusted, troubled by her brother's question. She feels sick. Her iPhone has been vibrating intermittently for the last twenty minutes. People are trying to speak to her, or one of her aliases, and it's rude not to respond. Picking up her iPhone, she notices Philip, intense eyes and gormless open mouth, staring at her, waiting for a response. Selina says, Fuck you. Communication is a right, we are all allowed to communicate. Another wave of sickness washes over her, and at this moment in time, everything in her life feels like a nightmare.

Philip smiles and asks Selina if she will make him a sandwich.

* * *

In the week post-graduation, Selina invited some friends to her parents' house for the weekend. Philip was away over both days and didn't meet any of them. Tom had stayed in the house and was getting along adequately with her friends. He thought they were mostly boring and career oriented, with nauseatingly limited commitment to pursuits. One of them, Ed, had given Tom a large bottle of San Miguel and struck up a conversation about mountain biking in the Alps during summer. Ed looked at Selina and said, He's alright. Which one is this?

Tom threw his San Miguel down on the patio, walked into the house and locked the door behind him.

* * *

Selina wraps her sandwich in cellophane and puts it inside a plastic ziplock. She is talking to herself, repeating a series of words over and over, mantra-like. Philip begins fidgeting, trying to get her attention. She puts the ziplock in the fridge, composes herself, and looks at him, What do you want?

You're making me feel excluded. When Tom dies I won't have anyone. We're not very close, I don't know, is that a problem for you?

I have a family, Philip. Did you have any idea that how I am now, before I had to come back to this house, is the healthiest I've ever been? How many times have you spoken to Meredith? No, please, I'm begging you to listen. You know that she can understand the conflict that exists between us. I'm trying to portray you and Tom as objectively as I can, but she knows, instinctively, the kind of people you are. I could have died, fucking died, when Tom locked me out of the house. It's an enclosed garden, it's en-close-d, there is lit-e-rally no o-th-er way out of there. He wanted me to die. Do you understand what it's like to know your brother tried to kill you?

Will you help me with my MA application?

* * *

Tom has lost two stone in weight and his head is clean shaven, revealing a small scar on his head, just above the tip of his ear, from a rock climbing accident dated one decade ago. Tom looks at Philip and explains how dying young is exactly the same as dying old.

Philip shakes his head and begins crying. Tom turns up the volume on the television. He gives Philip a handwritten list of instructions that relate to personal belongings and wishes for his non-future. He says, It's great, honestly.

Philip takes his t-shirt and trousers off and gets into the bed with Tom. They watch Homes Under The Hammer and then fall asleep facing each other, ready.

* * *

Philip logs on to Tom's Facebook. Someone called Carl, a friend from school, has written:

Goodbye Tom. Heavens Got There Best Angel Yet!!!1

Two hundred and fifty four people like the comment.

Philip stares at the screen for half an hour.

Philip deletes Carl as a friend and stares at the screen for half an hour, refreshing the page every thirty seconds.

Philip deletes all of Tom's friends, one by one.

Philip deactivates Tom's account, then his own.

Re-Hype The Like Machine

The course trains people to become teachers. The literature for the course application refers to passion and commitment and M-level certification. Some people get on the course at the first time of asking, others have to apply two or three times before they get on. Some people are joyous and enthusiastic and motivated by happiness, others are resigned and bored and motivated by fear. It has been said that this kind of mix is what makes a great group atmosphere.[1]

People have specialist subjects that they have spent three or more years studying. They have enough information to be able to pass on to other people. They can make PowerPoint presentations and talk about a specific aspect of a broader subject area. Their students will sit and look at the PowerPoint and sometimes ask questions or make notes.[2] The students will invite the teacher to sit with them in the cafeteria, whether the teacher chooses to do this or not is entirely at their discretion.

Someone says, Russell Group University. This is a lecturer speaking. A lecturer says, Russell Group Universities are, come on, Russell Group Universities are a significant step up, some

---

[1] Reference unavailable.
[2] In all likelihood, the students will not ask questions and will not make notes.

of you will find this, but don't worry, I'm sure you will be fine, yeah.

The lecturer says, Yeah, at the end of sixty to seventy percent of her sentences.[3] It's unclear whether this is knowing self-parody. The lecturer is disliked by fifty to sixty percent of the intake. The other forty to fifty percent like her. It is essential to have a concrete opinion on this. The lecturer starts talking about relationships. The lecturer says, There's always a hook up. It's funny that she uses the term hook up.

She repeats herself, this time louder, There's always a hook up, yeah.

People laugh. She says that there is always a relationship, sometimes a baby, and once a marriage. She says, Look at the people around you, sitting next to you, look them in the eyes. This is middle class bingo, yeah, and you're all playing, so—'

People start laughing again. People talk to the other people around them. People look around the lecture theatre as they talk to those sitting next to them. It is very loud in the lecture theatre now. There is screaming. A woman with blond hair and piercings on her face is saying, I've got a boyfriend, I've got a boyfriend, oh well, he's okay, he's okay, whatever.

The lecturer says, Calm down, you need to tune in. Yeah. You need to tune in.[4]

---

[3] Reference unavailable.

[4] Tuning in is important. If you don't tune in, you can't ever expect to be a course leader at M-level.

A woman with long dark hair rolls her eyes and looks sad. She is older, on average, than the other students. She is not enjoying herself. This is a difficult experience, she feels an urge to scald herself, to boil a kettle and spill some of the water on her leg. She picks up her iPhone and writes a Facebook status, immediately liking it.[5]

* * *

People on the course form bonds with each other. This is achieved via shared interests and cultural reference points. The most common cultural reference point is the television programme Peep Show. Peep Show is a long running situation comedy that is most notable for its distinctive aesthetic. The audience POV in Peep Show is unique in television programmes. We, the audience, us, see what the character talking sees. This means we, the audience, us, can watch the disappointment, surprise, or revulsion of others. We, the audience, us, can say things like:

I'm like that

Or

A comparable occurrence happened to me and I reacted in a similar manner.

---

[5] Reference unavailable.

This is a lie. We, the audience, us, are not involved in comparable occurrences and furthermore would not react in a similar way even if we were. We, the audience, us, are not similar to the characters on this television programme. We are paying thousands of pounds for M-level certification at a university for high achievers from affluent backgrounds; the characters on Peep Show live in a council flat and work boring, poorly paid jobs.

Geoff Davies can talk loudly, quickly, and for long periods of time without stopping. His political beliefs are:

moderate,

and his musical tastes are:

eclectic, anything good.

Geoff Davies trained to be an actor and won a third-year prize for his portrayal of Banquo in the play Macbeth by William Shakespeare; there is a video of the production on YouTube and it has thirty-five views and one thumbs up. His father is a GP[6] and happy that Geoff is training to become a teacher. Geoff is an only child and Jez is his favourite Peep Show character. This seems incongruous because to others, he is more of a Mark.

Kay Stevens is a raucous drunk, and this, in contrast to her brittle first impressions persona, affords her cult status

---

[6] Reference unavailable.

amongst her peers on the course. Kay is from Ohio but has lived in Wales for nine years. Kay is drinking Carling and saying, What, over and over. Kay says something about an ex-boyfriend and then something about daytime television before removing her cardigan and resting it on her arm. She is wearing a vintage T-shirt with Clinton 94 written on it.

Geoff is talking to Sarah, Megha[7] and Sophie.

Sophie is saying, I'm fucked, does someone want to buy some coke, or—

Geoff says, Goodbye, and walks over to the bar. He feels himself clamming up, ready to make a mess of everything. Kay is at the bar and they begin talking. They speak in disparaging terms of their course mates. Someone takes a photo of them and uploads it to Facebook. They both immediately like the photo.[8]

Upon completion of the course, having been in a relationship for four weeks, Geoff and Kay move in together. This makes sense.[9] It is the logical next step in their journey together and will fortify their brand. They Livestream their flat-warming party:

Is this everyone? Get the motherfucking Pringles out, Geoff.

---

[7] Megha faked some of her qualifications to get on the course (first time), Geoff (third time) felt angry and considered reporting this.
[8] The photo is genuinely a nice photo, totally unselfconscious and uninhibited.
[9] Reference unavailable.

Do I need to be worried about meeting your parents? Kay asks. She is smoking a cigarette, her face gaunt, lacklustre. Everything has been a struggle up to now. This relationship, the course, has been a respite, an upsurge of popularity and buzz around her brand. Kay puts out the cigarette and walks into the kitchen, Do I need to be worried about meeting your parents?

No, I don't think so. They'll like you. Don't use words like abortion or fuck or refer to reality TV[10] though, Geoff says. Geoff stands in front of the oven and checks that each hob is turned off. I think we should leave, we're running late. Should we go to Wagamama or Pizza Express? I think my parents booked somewhere, I don't know, Geoff says.

* * *

Inside the restaurant, Geoff's father says something about the importance of the NHS and Geoff agrees, violently, knocking over and partially spilling his drink. Kay takes a photo on her phone and everyone is suddenly very quiet. Geoff's father asks Kay if she enjoys photography.

No, why? Sorry, because I just took a photo. I—

---

[10] Geoff hated reality TV but enjoyed current affairs panel shows.

They leave the restaurant and take it in turns to hug each other. Geoff's father smiles as he hugs Geoff and smiles as he hugs Kay. Geoff's mother, appalled, smiles for the camera as her husband photographs her and Kay hugging. Geoff's mother is ambitious for Geoff,[11] but this is where her son is at, truly, in terms of:

his league.

Geoff's parents offer to let Geoff and Kay share a taxi back with them until their routes diverge. Kay stands still, her face neutral, hands by her sides. As his parents' taxi pulls away, Geoff says something about going to the museum.

Your parents are more orthodox than my parents. That's not a criticism. I'm not critiquing your parents, Kay says.

My dad just uploaded the photos onto his Facebook, Geoff says, Expect a friend request.

* * *

Kay reads her Facebook page going back over the last eight months. She is a popular person who can state an opinion and receive overwhelmingly positive responses from her friends. She can state an opinion in such a way that it is difficult for anyone (haters) to offer a contrary view (hating) without sounding aggressive or pathetically churlish. On average, a

---

[11] Geoff's mother believes ambition is crucial, the system works, we're in this together.

status will receive:

eleven likes,

fourteen comments.

On average, a photo will receive:

twenty-four likes,

nineteen comments.

Statistically, the most popular statuses and photos will be based on, or include, Geoff:

(Kay ~ Geoff synergy).

Kay looks up from her laptop, Do people talk about us, do they analyse our relationship, our sexual compatibility? Shut up. Which celebrity couple are we like? Are we like Ted and Sylvia? Tweet that. If a co-status gets less than ten likes then we're not doing our job properly, we're not doing it right, something is fucked up.

Please don't say celebrity couple, say famous couple, Geoff says. He struggled to match his middlebrow sensibilities to Kay's earnest interest in tabloid culture, but he did find her funny and liked how she expressed a preference for out-of-shape men. He, however, wished her body[12] and skin colour[13] was different and felt embarrassed at having previously

---

[12] Current: weak, very thin. Preferred: strong, curvy.
[13] Current: pallid. Preferred: caramel.

spoken of his appreciation for Brazilian women. He could never remember whether Kay had been there when he'd said it.[14] He thinks he should saying something. He does not say anything.

Kay began what would become a fifteen-minute monologue.

Geoff Googled Sofía Veraga Fake Bukakke.

* * *

There are four months lefts on the lease. Four months is not a long time. Four months is a series of workdays spaced around some weekends. The workdays can reduce contact time with the person you live with to a minimum. It depends. It's a workable option. Think about it and decide what it is you want. At weekends you can arrange interactions and these can be done with or without the person you live with.

There are four months left on the lease and nothing happens any more. Productivity and consumer engagement in the relationship is at an all time low. The flat is cold, the walls a dreary, dirty, shade of boring. Four months is the worst amount of time.

It's 6.30 p.m., eight weeks of relentless rain has seen an unprecedented level of distress inside the flat. Kay has been visiting the doctor three or four times a week. She is not eating.

---

[14] She hadn't.

She is smoking all day:

barely speaking.

She is smoking all day:

Loose Women is okay to look at.

Kay remembers the look on Geoff's mother's face the first time they met. She unfriends Geoff's mother.[15] She looks up at the ceiling, Do you remember when, um, no, should we write something, should we, should we sync a motherfucking profile picture rotation?

Re-hype the like machine, Geoff nods, teary eyed.

Squeezing her eyes shut as tightly as she can, she imagines blood seeping out the corner of each eye, gradually making its way down her face. The blood runs down her Insta-tinged face:

it's New Year's Eve[16] and a great time to demo your epic lifestyle—

---

[15] Kay had waited 2 x weeks and 1 x argument before accepting Geoff's mother's friend request.
[16] It isn't. It's January 27th.

Deleted Tweets

edited by @AmyRobots

feel like my body shape is / 'affluent gay man' / or russell crowe / dunno / lol /

wrote / deleted / wrote / 'inflammatory' anti-military comment for relative's facebook status / erdinger light /

GHGHGHGHGHGHGHG /

fixed narratives are good because you can stick to them /

all our shoes had holes in them / we came into money, we bought new shoes /

my wife is in the bath / 'am thinking about your face in my bum rn' / lol /

please don't ever forget about dre /

why do parents get mad when you try to explain pedagogy /

branding hard on tyskie / alone /

does woody allen know what xbox one is /

is it too late to be a yuppie /

when people complain about footballers' salaries they are implicitly endorsing media classism and racism / lol

hihihi, what up mitch winehouse /

idling on facebook / reporting offensive status' and comments like that's what's up / lol

richard gere, 'go home' [dies] / topher grace, 'okay' /

5AM: Hilton (Manchester, England)

The reception desk is made out of metal and glass. I want to touch it, but instead I step away from it. I'm not sure if I'm standing too far away. The woman behind the reception desk is maybe twenty-six or twenty-seven and wears a fitted blazer. I don't know about wearing a blazer. I want to say, Blazer, out loud and see how it sounds. The woman behind the reception desk starts talking to me.

I look at her eyes and her teeth and her lips. I tell her that I have lost the keycard for my room. She checks my details on a computer and tells me that a cleaner picked it up in the corridor and handed it in to her earlier. I say, That was lucky. I don't know if it was lucky or not. I am not sure what I mean. It is very difficult to focus and I look around for distractions. The lobby is quiet, a man and a woman sit on large taupe-coloured chairs and look at each other, smiling calmly and confidently at each other in synchronicity. I want them to look over to me so I can respond with a positive hand gesture, my contribution to the greater good.

The woman behind the reception desk asks me what I am doing this evening. I look at her eyes and her teeth and her lips. I tell her that I am going to lie down and read and maybe look at YouTube on my laptop. She tells me that they have an award-winning cocktail bar on the thirty-fifth floor and she can arrange a table for me and a guest. She looks at her watch and says, A guest, or—. I think that she wants to have a cocktail with me and get to know the real me and have a twelve to eighteen month relationship. After twelve to eighteen months, she will reassess her life and the kind of man she wants to be with. That man will not be me, but that's okay, none of this has happened yet.

I tell the woman behind the reception desk that I have an early start filming tomorrow and shouldn't drink. Her eyes glaze over and she falls silent, her head titling to the side as if in standby mode. If I say something I don't know whether she will respond. She appears neutral, peaceful.

The lobby is suddenly full and behind me a group of maybe fifteen people queue to gain access to the lift and the thirty-fifth floor cocktail bar. They are making a lot of noise. I turn and recognise some of them from television; they all seem to be enjoying themselves and then one of them, a woman who is best known for shitting herself, starts shouting and crying. I turn away and look at the woman behind the desk. She remains motionless and if I want her to respond I'll have to speak louder than I like to. I decide that I don't want to speak at all.

* * *

I walk into the room and am surprised by how warm it is. The room knows that it's cold outside and I don't own a winter coat. Some people own a winter coat, some people own more than one winter coat. It doesn't matter, the room knew I would

103

be cold and it turned the heating up for me. I feel that staying warm is important. My father used to lie in front of the fire in the living space, and if I was cold he would let me lie on top of him, so we both got warm.

He was a kind and agreeable old cheetah.
He was a prickly and irritable old cheetah.
He was a cheetah because he was slim and could run fast.
He was an old cheetah because he was old and he was a cheetah.

Cheetah anecdote:

An old cheetah was lying in front of the fire in the living space and I snuck up behind with the intention to generate feelings of surprise and humour. The old cheetah quickly turned around and drew back his paw as if he was going to swipe me away. The old cheetah had an earnestly angry facial expression. I felt myself go pale. I felt myself starting to cry. I ran from the living space and into the craft area, hearing the cheetah shouting about how he was joking and I was a baby with no sense of humour. I hid behind the kiln with my head in my hands, thinking about how I could make clay spears to kill the cheetah with.

The room knew I would be cold and acted accordingly. The room doesn't know how many coats I do or don't own, or the impact of my cheetah experiences. I lie on the bed and open my laptop.

Google:

reincarnation as a dickhead jungle cat—

reincarnation as womb era Suri Cruise—

reincarnation as Friends complete series DVD boxset—

reincarnation as fairtrade sex based on humour, mutual attraction, amanda bynes, non exploitative booty—

Come twice.

Watch YouTube videos of Call of Duty multiplayer team deathmatches.
Watch YouTube videos of dolphins being born.
Watch YouTube videos of Jeremy Beadle making baked beans fly everywhere.
Watch YouTube videos of Jeremy Beadle making cars fall into lakes.

I think about whether Jeremy Beadle ever took things too far. Did he ever cause true anguish that led to unpredictable and heartbreakingly catastrophic results? I don't know whether this would be a problem for him given that his commitment to the craft was believed to be at levels beyond sane comprehension. I'm not being honest with myself: I don't care if he hurt people, I only care about the out-of-control spinning vats of baked beans.

I get up from the bed and walk over to the clear glass wall that looks out onto some bars, the tram line, and, further afield, poor suburbs and rich suburbs.

The rich suburbs mostly contain white people or people who aspire to be perceived as white by white people. There are too many rich white people and not enough houses which leads to the prices becoming prohibitive even for them. Some of the rich white people will look on the internet and find places they can move to in the poor suburbs. With the right amount of money it is very easy to:

Rip out a kitchen.
Knock through a living room.
Murder an upstairs.
Rim a garden.

This will make the house worth more money. This is great. This will mean they can one day move to the rich suburb they wanted in the first place. The poor people will all be homeless and irrelevant, with only their social media presence and unreliable wifi to comfort them as they ride the tram until they die.

I am on the thirty-first floor. I can see the rich suburbs and the poor suburbs. No one is entirely happy. I want to move to Mars on the back of an iconic triumph that will never be forgotten.

I am on the thirty-first floor. I am thirty-one floors closer to Mars than most people.

I am on the thirty-first floor. I am vulnerable to a terror attack. This thought makes me laugh. If a plane hit the building, or a bomb went off and the structure started to collapse, I would not move. I would stay standing in front of the clear glass wall and listen to people screaming and watch the crowds gathering. Television crews would arrive and try to win prestigious prizes for their coverage. They would bring their best equipment. Standing still in the window, I would keep smiling and maybe go viral.

It's okay, everything is going to be fine. Embrace your inevitable and potentially exciting death environment. Terror is the sole exciting activity that remains in the world.

It's okay, everything is going to be fine. I'm going to die, but I'm being reincarnated as a happy-go-lucky sloth gif with a what's for dinner? attitude.

I walk over to the bed and lie down.

I close my eyes and think about a hybrid wheatgrass-heroin shot. I fall asleep.

I wake up and feel as if none of this has happened yet, that I'm waiting for something, anything.

I want concrete results and I want them yesterday.

I don't know where I am.

I remember a robot. She worked behind a reception desk and had nice eyes, teeth, and lips. I hope she is happy and not experiencing any physical or existential crises.

It's dark, I can't see anything. I look at my iPhone for between thirty seconds and a minute. I look at my Gmail and continuously refresh the screen for between thirty seconds and a minute.

Welcome to the beginning of a glorious career.

None of this has happened yet.

Party / Keep It All Together

I arrive home from work and Jaimie asks how my day was. I tell Jaimie that I am on a career path and nothing can stop me from achieving my goals going forwards. Jaimie looks sad and says, Don't worry.

I go for a shower. The shower-head is large and purports to affect the impact of a monsoon or waterfall or some kind of extreme water experience. The water hits my head and a dozen individual drops continue down and onto my shoulders. I shout, The shower again, and wait for a reply. I turn up the heat. I turn down the heat. I reach for the fifteen-year-old towel hanging from the bathroom door.

Jaimie shouts, I don't think the shower's working properly, FYI—

* * *

My sister calls and tells me that my mother is in hospital, stable but under observation. She explains that my mother fell from the roof of her house and probably would have died except that her fall was broken by a water butt.

I ask my sister to explain to me what a water butt does. I ask my sister for a history of water butts.

I ask my sister to describe what a water butt looks like and whether it can have variations in its appearance, size, and or shape.

My sister says that she cannot answer my questions.

I say, Terse, and ask my sister whether there is a Wikipedia entry for water butts.

My sister says that she does not know whether there is a Wikipedia entry for water butts and tells me that I need to go and see my mother in hospital. My sister sounds angry.

I say, Water butts.

My sister hangs up the phone.

I pick up my cat and look her in the eyes. I think, Water butts. My cat laughs and says, No, seriously, water butts are water tanks used to collect and store rainwater runoff, typically from rooftops via rain gutters. They are devices for collecting and maintaining harvest rain. They are installed to make use of rainwater for later use, reduce mains water use for economic or environmental reasons, and aid self-sufficiency. Stored water may be used for watering gardens, agriculture, flushing toilets, in washing machines, washing cars, and also for drinking, especially when other water supplies are unavailable, expensive, or of poor quality. In ground they can also be used for retention of stormwater for release at a later time. In arid climates, they are often used to store water during the rainy season for use during drier periods. With tanks used for drinking water, the user runs a health risk if maintenance is not carried out. My cat's voice sounds like Julia Stiles in every Julia Stiles film. She wriggles out of my arms and jumps onto the sofa, immediately falling asleep. She is content, she understands the inherent privilege of knowledge and also enjoying a free ride.

I open my laptop and search for cheap return train tickets so I can go and see my mother in hospital. There are no cheap train tickets. If I want to use the train to go and see my mother and then return to where I live, it will cost me one hundred and sixty-five pounds, taking four and a half hours each way.

I search for cheap return coach fares so that I can go and see my mother. I find coach fares that will cost me forty-seven pounds in total. I think:

Seems reasonable.

I look at the journey details and see that the coach will take nine hours each way. I think:

Feel furiously angry and disturbed by this twist.

I walk to the kitchen and fill a pint glass with tap water. I feel calm. I look into the garden and some of the washing has detached from the clothes line and is lying in the flower bed. I think:

You are feeling calm. Also, you are sweating.

I walk back to the laptop and search for return flights so that I can go and see my mother. I find flights that cost sixty pounds each way and take less than one hour. I complete the purchase of the tickets and walk to the kitchen and fill a pint glass with tap water. I drink the pint in one go and hope for positive outcomes.

* * *

This is my mother's eleventh recorded suicide attempt. I open a Word document entitled Oh No:

August 2012 / roof jump, injuries unknown, saved by recycling bin and water butt, informed by sister via phn call /

I highlight water butt and change the font to Comic Sans.

My mother's first recorded suicide attempt took place in her car and occurred six months after my father disappeared.

My mother's second recorded suicide attempt took place on the roof of her house.

My mother's third recorded suicide attempt took place in the attic room of her house.

My mother's fourth recorded suicide attempt took place in the greenhouse in her garden.

My mother's fifth recorded suicide attempt took place in the bedroom of her house.

My mother's sixth recorded suicide attempt took place on the roof of her house.

My mother's seventh recorded suicide attempt took place on the roof of her house.

My mother's eighth recorded suicide attempt took place on the roof of her house.

My mother's ninth recorded suicide attempt took place during the viewing of a house she was interested in buying.

My mother's tenth recorded suicide attempt took place above an open manhole.

My mother's eleventh recorded suicide attempt took place inside a wasp's nest.

I close the document and save the changes.

I walk upstairs and begin packing an overnight bag.

My cat follows me and falls asleep on the bed.

I email work from my iPhone and tell them I need an indefinite amount of time off from work, effective immediately, so I can visit my suicidal mother. They reply but I delete the email, unread.

* * *

Jaimie parks the car. Jaimie turns her head to look at me. Jaimie bites her bottom lip with her two front teeth and says, Beaver thugs for life.

Jaimie says, You look sad.

I say, Sad beaver.

Jaimie says, Don't be sad, beaver.

I reach over and pull my overnight bag into the front seat. I look at my iPhone.

Jaimie puts her hands on either side of her head, twitches them, and makes bleepy-bloopy radar noises, Mingus cat is sending you a message. She says everything is okay, everything is fine.

I get out of the car.

* * *

I board the plane. The plane is being piloted by two German men. They seem like positive individuals who know when to party and when to keep it all together. The plane is so small the cockpit is not separated from the passenger seating area. We are in this together. The plane gathers speed on the runway. The plane takes off. There are no spare seats on the plane. We are in this together. I take my iPod out of my jacket pocket and put Colossal Youth on repeat. I close my eyes.

* * *

I open my eyes. The pilots are talking to each other, smiling. Sometimes, they press buttons. Most of the time they just look straight ahead, grinning.

I close my eyes.

* * *

I get out of the taxi and my mother is in the driveway. She is wearing a neck-brace and is lifting a butler sink into an old, rusty wheelbarrow with a flat front wheel. We go inside. She asks if I want a panad. I say yes. She asks if I still drink milk. I

113

say yes. We talk about everything, solidly, for one hour. I eat a packet of ready salted crisps. I eat half a packet of digestive biscuits. My mother tells me that the neck-brace will be coming off in six to eight weeks but there's no way that it's stopping her from doing her craft or garden activities. I ask her why she checked herself out of the hospital. I try to not sound angry. I ask her why she was lifting a sink when I arrived. I try to not sound angry. She looks at me and tells me that she was lifting the sink because the sink needed lifting and she couldn't wait for people to move it for her. I shake my head and try to not look angry. I look at the newspaper on the kitchen table. I tell her she should read a better newspaper. She stares out of the window for a moment, then says that we're having vegetarian lasagne for tea. She asks if I still eat vegetarian lasagne. I tell her that I still eat vegetarian lasagne. She smiles and holds my hand. She kisses my hand and then sticks her tongue out at me.

I'm going out tonight, Mam. With Cal. And later with some other people.

Okay, don't be too late. I'll leave the back door open.

No, Jesus, don't do that. I have a key, I say, feeling simultaneously anxious, angry, and amused.

I get up from the table and pour tap water into a pint glass.

* * *

It's cold outside the club; it's been raining and when a woman falls over into a puddle people cheer. A man in his forties starts a modified version of a popular terrace chant: She falls where she wants. It is difficult to tell for sure, but the fallen woman is laughing rather than crying as she struggles to get back on her feet. Another woman helps her up and raises her arm above her head to cheers from a handful of people.

I look at my iPhone.

A man asks me if he can borrow twenty pence. I give the man twenty pence. The man says thank you and asks if he can borrow ninety pence. I give the man ninety pence and the man says thank you and asks if he can borrow seventy pence. I give the man seventy pence and the man asks if I have any more money that he can borrow. I don't know what to say. The man is looking at me, waiting. I tell the man that I don't know what to say. The man walks away from me.

I look at my iPhone.

I feel unable to process anything that is going on around me. I can't read the time. I think it says 2.45 a.m. I can't make out whether the two is a two. I can't discount it being a one, a three, or a four.

Someone is talking to me. I think I went to school with this person. He is talking to me like he knows me. I think he got my name right. I tell him that I have nothing in common with anyone I went to school with. He says something and a woman walks over. She is called Sarah and I think I went to school with her. She asks me if I heard about Jason Rhys. I tell her that she looks different to how she did in school. She says

Jason Rhys four or five times and has an angry facial expression. I laugh and say that out of everyone from school, Jason Rhys is the one person I concretely know that I have things in common with. And that's funny because he's a convicted sex offender, I say, laughing.

The man says, I don't, what, um, you can't, but, what, um—

Sarah looks angry and keeps repeating the same thing, over and over, something about:

A Disgrace Gone Mad.

I say, He's not a paedophile durrr, Jesus, fucking stupid, sorry I'm drunk, but—

The man starts shouting and Sarah starts shouting. It is very loud. Some other people have come over and are shouting.

I say, Sorry, bye, and run away.

I think, I'm jogging rather than flat-out sprinting.

I fall over and land in a puddle. I think:

Feel like this will be funny in retrospect

I get up and carry on jogging.

I stop jogging. I don't know where I am. I am drunk, but less drunk than twenty minutes ago. I look at my iPhone. It is 3.45 a.m. I put my hand in my pockets and look at how much money I have. I do not have enough money for a taxi home.

It's okay. I am going to jog home. In my spare time I enjoy going to clubs, jogging home, and trying new foods from around the world. I'm a meticulously well-rounded individual with a positive future. I think:

Is five miles the same as five kilometres?

I start jogging.
I stop jogging and throw up on the pavement.
I walk for half an hour.
I start jogging.
I stop jogging.
I walk across a bridge and think:

Grew up on an island.

I start jogging. I jog past my childhood home and think:

Open-plan living. I don't know.

I stop jogging.

I look at my iPhone. It is 5.30 a.m. I can hear a very loud car engine in the distance. I look up at the road lights and some of them aren't working. I look down at the pavement and feel like I'm walking on a plank of rotting wood and may fall into the earth without warning. I can hear a very loud car engine. I can't see any headlights. I look up at the sky.

I look at my iPhone. A car with no headlights drives past me. I turn around to look at the car. The car flips over. The car is in the air, floating or flying or something. The car hits a tree.

The top half of the car is on one side of the tree.

The bottom half of the car is on the other side of the tree.

Now there are two half-cars.

I walk over to the half-cars. I walk over to the tree. I look at the half-cars. I look at the tree.

There is a human head on the floor. The eyes are open. I walk over to the human head and say, Can you hear me?

The human head's eyes blink. The human head has broken cheekbones and fractured eye-sockets and is covering itself in blood, relentlessly. The human head's eyes blink again.

What's it like? Blink if it feels hopeful, I say.

The human head does not blink. The human head has a broken jaw and is missing one ear and is spurting blood over the floor and over my shoes. The human head's lip trembles.

I'm going to call an ambulance, I say.

The human head starts laughing.

I'm going to call an ambulance and then follow you on Twitter, I say.

The human head is laughing.

I look at the human head. I look at my iPhone and dial 999. I tell the operator that I need the police and an ambulance. The operator tells me to expect a twenty minute wait, and I relay this to the head. The human head's lips start trembling, or maybe spasming. The human head starts screaming.

Sorry, bye, I say.

I take my iPhone out of my pocket and put on Seinwave 2000 by /\belard at full volume. Holding the iPhone to my ear, I start jogging and don't stop until I arrive at my mother's house.

* * *

I open the back door and walk through the porch into the kitchen.

I open a cupboard and look at small plastic bottles.

I look at the paintings on the walls and the plastic cereal containers on the shelves.
I open a tube of Pringles and eat half.
I open a carton of Tropicana and drink half.
I pick up a block of Applewood cheese and take three bites.
I pick up falafel from a small plastic container and take two bites.
I take my iPhone out of my pocket and write Jaimie a text.
I look at my iPhone for two-three-four-five minutes, pressing the home button every thirty seconds to refresh the screen light.
I look at a Christmas cake.
I eat Christmas cake icing.
I go to the toilet and throw up for twenty minutes.

My mother shouts, Are you okay?

I shout, I'm fine. Are you okay?

My mother shouts, I'm okay. I got your email, I forgot to say before, I can give you some money.

I shout, I'm paying it back. Please don't die before I pay it back.

All The Places We Lived (Part 3 of 3)

Day -177:

Noah changed his name to Osian.

Jess changed her name to Catrin.

Osian and Catrin bought a new house together. The house had enough space for two people, two average- to small-sized people. The previous owner had died in the house. It was unclear whether he had died in the bathroom, the bedroom, the garden, or wherever – but he was dead and the house was made available for sale. When a house is made available for sale it has an asking price. You can offer less than the asking price and see if that works. The agent might say:

Um, no, the vendor is after a little bit more than that.

Or the agent could say:

I'll have to check, but I think that is a great offer.

How you interpret these responses is up to you. You can decipher any subtext, mindfucking tactics, or uncertainty on the part of the agent. You can do whatever you like, but if you want the house you should be ready and calm and determined:

I am ready to conclude this by the end of play today.

It's okay to say 'end of play' to an agent, because this is what they understand and in their eyes you become a credible option when you demonstrate a willingness to assimilate yourself amongst the sewage.

The decor inside the house was okay; it was plain and dated, the artex walls a reminder that almost everyone reaches a point where improvement is no longer a consideration and it's okay to exist and not give a shit. This can be a moment of joy, or of sadness. It's up to you.

Osian folded the stanley knife and looked at the living-room wall, scored and ready to be steamed. I feel uncomfortable that people, our neighbours, will see us renovating and think we're here to make money or something, he said.

I don't think our neighbours will think that. I don't think anyone would think that about us. You look handsome, Catrin said. She undid the buttons on either side of her green denim dungaree top—

* * *

Day -121:

Catrin was drinking with her friend, Petra. They had been drinking since half four.

Osian was drinking with his friend Dave, his friend Kier, and his friend Rob. They had been drinking since half one, maybe two.

It was three in the morning and Osian texted Catrin to say that he wanted to go home, he was ready to go home, he was going to get a burger and then go home. Catrin texted back to say:

Okay, call me. I'm outside O'Malley's.

Osian said goodbye to Dave, goodbye to Kier, goodbye to Rob. Rob couldn't hear him though. Rob had a bad ear and used a hearing aid during the day but never wore it out at night; he said it meant he had to listen to a little less bullshit.

Osian looked at his iPhone and felt compelled to get something to eat alone before he got something to eat with Catrin. Burger King was full of people, everyone was shouting at the Sri Lankan men behind the counter; they seemed distantly amused as they relayed the orders to the Polish men behind them in the kitchen area.

Osian was at the front of the queue. Does this one have pork in it? he said, pointing at a flatscreen above the Sri Lankan man's head. No? Okay, I'll have that one please. Diolch.

The Sri Lankan man smiled, warmly, calmly, Diolch yn fawr.

The seating area was full except for the barstools that faced the street outside. Osian sat down and opened up the burger packaging. He looked at the open packet and thought:

This is well put together.

Osian looked at the burger and thought:

I am a disgusting human being.

Osian ate the burger then walked up to the counter and asked for another of the same burger. The Sri Lankan man readjusted his baseball hat, then his glasses, and said, Um, okay, diolch, sir, diolch yn fawr iawn.

* * *

Catrin was standing in the doorway outside of O'Malley's. She was talking to a man in a green Fred Perry overcoat. She was looking at her iPhone, smiling how she smiled when she was bored or unimpressed. She was:

trying to end the conversation with the man in the green Fred Perry overcoat.

Osian approached Catrin and from maybe thirty metres away saw her talking to the man in a green Fred Perry overcoat. She was looking at her iPhone, smiling how she smiled when she was drunkenly horny. She was:

typing the man in the green Fred Perry coat's number into her contacts—

* * *

Day -120:

Osian poured Catrin half a pint of kale, cucumber, kiwi and apple smoothie. He brought it up to the bedroom and left it on the bedside table.

Where are you going? Catrin said, hazily, her voice croaking.

Um.

We're bringing out the worst in each other—

Um. I don't, um—

You threw a fucking burger at my head, Catrin said, taking a small sip of the smoothie.

I threw a burger at your head because you punched me in the stomach, dickhead.

Catrin sat up in the bed and took a large gulp of the juice. You shouldn't use words like that, it's so aggressive. You're always so aggressive. I had mayonnaise in my hair. The taxi driver asked if a bird had crapped on me.

Oh. I don't know.

We can't keep doing this.

Okay, we'll stop. Just tell me what to do. Let me tell you what to do. I honestly have a future planned, for us. I think it just, I don't know sometimes it's difficult to concentrate. I find it difficult to concentrate. That's not the only thing I find difficult—

I want you to trust me. You don't trust me. It's because we've been together, and we were young, but I'm not immature, I understand you... I'm so sorry. I'm not the person who punched you.

I know, I know you're not. I'm not the person who threw the burger—

Lol, you are. But you're not the person who threw the burger at me.

I'll always be the person who throws the burgers, but I'll never be the person who throws the burgers at you.

Catrin took another sip from the smoothie and held it out for Osian. Osian climbed into the bed, took a sip from the juice and pressed his nose into Catrin's ear—

* * *

Day -23:

Osian had been temping with an organisation, an international education provider called the BSO, for several months, and had interviewed unsuccessfully twice during this time for permanent positions. It seemed like an okay place to be and the renovations on the house needed to be paid for. Osian spent a lot of time in the building:

in the ground floor toilet,

walking up and down corridors carrying blank pieces of paper,

finding conference rooms with unguarded cheese wheels inside them,

in the third floor toilet eating cheese wheels.

It was an okay place to be. The house renovations needed to be paid for.

The summer was the busiest time of the year. The hopes of two million students hung in the balance as their exam papers were marked and processed. This was called The Session and Osian's colleagues enjoyed the increased level of pressure, the adrenalin, the heightened importance afforded to straightforward administrative tasks.

A permanent position came up again and Osian applied. The only difference in his interview, at least that he was conscious of, was how he repeated the organisation's mantra at the beginning and end of each answer:

I believe in the BSO's mission, and that mission is education.

The interview panel nodded their heads and ticked boxes. Osian demonstrated competency scores that ranged from adequate to good. He was awarded a full-time permanent position with a salary and paid holiday and sick leave.

Day -17:

I'm getting married next week, I'll need eight days off. We booked the honeymoon, it's all paid for, Osian said, calmly, grinning.

That's fine. You'll need to make up the time when you get back, Rod said. Rod was Osian's line manager. He was younger than Osian but looked a lot older. He had bad digestion and his dreadful bowels often ruined Osian's visits to the toilet.

Okay. I will do that. That is fine. I will do that, Osian said. He sat down at his desk and looked at Medium.com for two hours. He looked at an article about how to make jam. He looked at an article about Xbox One. He looked at an article about Nothing Was The Same.

Osian looked at his phone, there was one hour before he could leave. He stood up from his desk, walked through the double doors at the south facing end of the office and turned left into the toilet.

Day -3:

How are you getting on with your emails? Rod asked. Rod had returned from a smoking break with one of his bosses. He seemed excited, aggressive somehow.

Oh, great.

Osian deleted two hundred unread emails from his inbox. It felt like the interesting thing to do, the option that inspired him the most. He thought:

It's important to feel inspired, to feel interested and stimulated.

He wondered whether the people would email back in a few days and how polite, or not, they would be; he wanted to investigate how far he could test their patience in the face of a ticking clock and numerical objectives and targets. Osian took a photo of his hand in the thumbs-up position and WhatsApp'd it to his friend Prune:

T-Up for the office lifestyle.

Day -2:

Osian put the building security fob inside the top drawer and began tidying his desk. People all around him were walking and talking. It was just like The West Wing.

Osian finished tidying. His was a desk of a confident and charming young sociopath, ready to maintain the momentum from his interview, take it through The Session, and come out on the other side primed for training opportunities that could only end up in management opportunities. He believed in the mission, and that mission was education. Osian's phone rang. He picked it up and said:

No—

[##########]

I don't think so—

[##########].

I don't know who Oh-si-un is—

[##########]

129

Okay, no—

[#########]

Okay, no—

[#########]

Okay, no problem, I'll tell Oh-si-un, whoever that is. Bye—

[#########]

Bye—

[#########]

[#########]

[#########]

[#########]

Bye—

Day 0:

I just think, if you're going to quit a job you need to tell me.
We're supposed to be a team. I'm your wife. I'm really fucking
angry with you. Why couldn't you have just gone off sick for a
month until you got another job?

Oh—

Day 6:

I have a job holding up a billboard. I can pretend to sign people up for PPI claims and I get paid six hundred pounds a week.

Ok, lol. I Love you, Catrin said, grinning, rubbing her nose. I love you Billboard Man. But—

I know. I learnt my lesson. The whole point of how we live is that we can do what we feel like, and I felt like quitting the job. I wanted to do something like that. It made me laugh. I'd finally broken into a career and could be earning a lot of money in a couple of years, and the opportunity to throw that away was just too good to, um, throw away. Also, I felt it was a compelling narrative arc for my character. Who saw that coming? I thought of it in those exact terms when the idea came into my head. Compelling narrative arc. Imagine that.

But—

No, I do know. We can do what we want, but we need to think about the other person too. Not the other people in the fucking job, but the other person like you. You: the other person. I love you. You're my other person. I love you—

Catrin smiled, shook her head. Catrin smiled, nodded her head. Catrin said, We should try for a baby. I'm really into that idea at the moment.

Day 16:

You are happier than I have ever known you, Osian.

You are happier than I have ever known you, Catrin.

Osian handed Catrin an orange, celery, carrot and ginger smoothie. He took the straw out of his plastic container and removed the lid. He lifted the container up to his lips and drank half. He smiled. He lifted the container up to his lips and drank the other half. Oh God, I drank that too quickly, he said, his eyes watering.

Catrin laughed, I meant it.

What?

All of it. The whole time.

* * *

Day 1250 (approx):

They lived in the house for longer than they had ever lived anywhere. They adapted and improved the space to suit them, first to suit their aesthetic preferences.

Then to suit their pets.

Then to suit their children.

Sun Tree by Terry Frost hung above the table in the living room. It's important to know that Sun Tree comprises of circles, rectangles, hearts in red, orange, blue, yellow, purple. You can buy prints of it if that's what you want to do. If you buy it you can hang it on a wall in your home and look at it. You can look at it and understand it and think about what motivates you, what inspires you, what makes you smile. You can do what you like.

Osian and Catrin stood in front of the table. Osian wore a white T-shirt, black Cheap Monday jeans, barefoot. Catrin wore a blue Frances Ha custom breast pocket Pocketeers t-shirt, black leggings, barefoot.

Osian looked at Catrin and then at Sun Tree, This is beautiful to me. Feels like all the places we lived.

Explicit / Rare Communications

Kanye

Kim, I feel uncomfortable with the role attributed to me within your family. I am not happy being viewed as a person who makes strange or eccentric comments. I am a serious person who thinks critically and analytically. It is very strange for me to have to inhabit the role of comedian or clown. In no other company am I treated this way. I'm not trying to scare anyone or make anyone feel uncomfortable. I understand that your family have a set narrativisation of the world that has worked for them, certainly from a financial point of view, but also societally – and there is a guttural suspicion of any challenging of this. This is alien to me. This is alien because I challenge everything and enjoy the process. Maybe this is because I have had far less to lose. I had nothing materially, I was always a talented and intelligent person. You knew this. Everything I say is treated with suspicion, even when I am I speaking factually. The most obnoxious culprit is Scott; when I said that Einstein and Da Vinci were vegetarian he took it very personally for some reason. He raised his voice and cursed. Kourtney looked nervous and hushed him. She does this often. Scott couldn't look me in the eyes, it was unclear who he was addressing. It's okay, I understand why Scott is the way he is. You are barely related, I don't care, he is a very miserable person. He is crass. His lack of self-awareness and intelligence explains why he places so much emphasis on monetary and material success. It is a shame because he, like me, has married out of his class or race or whatever. In that respect we are similar and these are the foundations that can lead to people becoming friends. He does not want to be my friend. **That's okay**. I won't try to be his friend anymore. I shouldn't care so much, but I'm sensitive. In that respect I am envious of Scott. His wilfully ignorant view of the world acts as a shield to circumnavigate the need for dealing with any meaningful level of emotion. I want this noted: during a party I overheard two of his peers describe him as 'ambitious', the connotations being explicitly negative and mocking. I am not ambitious in that sense. I am attracted to your face and your body (you are made out of butter for God's sake) and you make me laugh and we talk at length, and with sophistication, about a variety of subjects. I've seen Kourtney stiffening with embarrassment when Scott speaks. I don't know, maybe this is not accurate, but I think a disproportionate amount of time has been spent between the two of them discussing me in negative contexts. Kourtney is okay, but she is bored a lot of the time. I think she bores herself or she has come to accept boredom. What do Kourtney and Scott talk about? Fuck.

I have moved from the hotel, I am writing this from a small attic. It has rained every day since I have been here but **even that is glorious to me**.

I will write you another letter this evening maybe.

Kanye

I'm worried about my family. They won't listen to me or ask for help. I don't understand this. I'm not ashamed, or embarrassed, to say that I know better. I'm just being honest and when they get angry it baffles me. It's easy to block me on Facebook, refuse to take my calls, but I'm the only person in their life speaking the truth. The only one who'll tell the truth at their funeral or their murder trial or their whatever wherever. No one knows my family exists. **I know they exist, Kim**. No one else knows, and no one will ever know. They don't understand that you can change things about your life that you don't like or make you feel bad. When people fetishise their suffering, I mean people do this (not just my family, but people in similar situations), it only encourages others, like family, friends, social workers, whoever, to accept it as the only option. I'm worried because if they're dying, or going crazy, or not stopping each other from dying or going crazy, then it's all on me and I won't be encouraged or even allowed to help. People in poverty can be offered something better but they won't choose it because it might, in their heads, mean they lose what they have at that moment. **Wow**. That's not my original idea. It's credible scholarship, I just can't remember who wrote it. I tried Googling it. I'm going to keep on trying to find it, because it's important. What I'm doing is important.

I just thought: this temperature is just right. I am looking up and the ceiling window is clear.

I am looking at a star. I think it's moving.

I can't sleep.

Kanye

I went to the Pompidou, hoping it would be incredible. **It was** incredible. I sat outside and felt anger at not having been exposed to this aspect of culture as a child. I have had to teach myself things, but it's not enough to know facts or dates or even entire transcripts unless you feel comfortable and relaxed when you talk about them, like: it's no big deal I know this, this is normal, this is something you would expect me to know and be able to talk about. People are sometimes surprised when I talk about certain things, like pedagogy or post-structuralism, and that in itself, the look on their face, however subtle, but always intentional, is an assault on my person. **An assault on my person, Kim**. I've wasted a lot of time, some of it has been wasted on my behalf. I have always been uncomfortable or at odds with something during my life. I don't know, it's too obvious to say that this is why I have expressed myself the way I have expressed myself. I thought about when my mother died and how it made me produce something amazing and then I thought about what I would make if you died.

I don't want you to die.

I don't want you to die.

I don't want you to die.

It rained this afternoon, everyone seemed okay about that. All of the umbrellas are black here. Feel like: why has no one designed an umbrella that catches rainwater and just does something awesome with that water. I want to invent that umbrella, Kim.

I'm going to write to you again later.

Kanye

It was sunny, maybe a little humid, on Thursday. I took the metro to Montmartre. I started talking to a man, he had an open day at his studio, he was a carpenter, or cabinet maker – I'm not sure which, but he told me the difference, and it's an important difference. We were talking and he told me about his family, his wife and kids. How he communicated his feelings so clearly, how he was able to explain himself so calmly, even the deepest things. I felt tearful, he told me it was okay to cry. I couldn't cry, he told me that was okay too. We spoke for three hours and drank camomile tea. He told me he was an open person who liked to tell people how he felt. He told me that he liked me, that instinctively he felt as if we had much in common, shared sensibilities, similarities in our upbringings. He continued to say that when this happens, it's important to make sure you are honest and unequivocal with the other person: I like you and want to be your friend, let's ensure that this happens. We exchanged emails and hugged. It felt good and I smiled all the way back to the city. I want you to download Julia With Blue Jeans On by Moonface.

I miss you.

Kanye

What is the biggest danger to our daughter, to all our kids, in the future? The biggest danger that might screw it all up for everyone. I don't know, but I am trying to figure it out.

I don't want to believe it could ever be me.

I hope it's not us.

I can't believe it would be us.

If we're having sex and you only come once, am I happy with that? I'm an extremist. I don't know, I suppose it just depends on how I'm feeling. I've given up on the moderate approach, I don't think it works. I don't know if it... what I mean by moderate approach, approach to what, well; approach to work, politics, or any aspect of how I live. How we live. Any aspect. The moderate approach is what stops advancement, and it's a deliberate and insidious way of thinking perpetuated:

by people
by people
by people
by people.

We're not those people.

We're not those people, Kim, **and if I can't transmit these explicit / rare communications to you, if not you—**

Kim

Kim is typing

Kim is offline

Kim is offline

Kim is offline

Kim is offline

Kim is offline

Kim is offline

Kim is offline

Kim is offline

Kim is offline

Kim is offline

Kim is offline

Kim is offline

Kim is offline

Kim is offline

Kim is offline

Kim is offline

Kim is offline

Kim is offline

Kim is offline

Kim is offline

Kim is offline

Kim is offline

Kim is offline

Kim is offline

Kim is offline

Kim is typing

Index

Acknowledgements

Thank you to Susie Wild and Richard Davies at Parthian Books, Amy Roberts, Carys Roberts, Jim Friel, Alicia Stubbersfield, Prune Campbell, Chapter Arts Centre, Erdinger Light, Vegetarian Food Studio, and wheatgrass shots.

More short-story collections from...

PARTHIAN